Margaret at Barnard

Also by R. L. Rhyse

Margaret of Greenwich

Margaret and Erika

Margaret at War

Margaret in Tokyo

Margaret and Eve

Margaret and Velda

Margaret and Emily

Margaret and Hillary

Margaret in London

Margaret of Greenwich

R. L. Rhyse

Margaret at Barnard

Book Ten in the
Margaret of Greenwich® Series

Wyston Books, Inc.

Margaret of Greenwich

Wyston Books, Inc.

www.margaretofgreenwich.com
www.wystonbooks.com

R. L. Rhyse
Margaret at Barnard: a novel
Book Ten in the Margaret of Greenwich® Series

1. Margaret of Greenwich (Fictitious character)
2. Teenage Girls Fiction

Library of Congress Control Number: 2015943925
ISBN 978-0-9903920-4-0
EISBN 978-0-9903920-5-7
Cover Photograph by UpperCut Images/
Licensed from Getty Images
BISAC: JUV014000 (Girls & Women)
JUV028000 (Mysteries & Detective Stories)
JUV026000 (Love & Romance)

Growing up means learning
to be yourself all over again.
—Margaret

If you must battle, it is important
to choose the time and the place.
—Margaret

Margaret of Greenwich

CHAPTER 1

I hunted through my roommate's underwear drawer for the tampons that I needed and she said were there. Within the Playtex Sport Fresh Balance Tampon box lay two surprises. The first was a "female friendly" purple and black pistol. These colorful guns have surged in sales to women for self-defense.

The second surprise was a cigarette lighter. Missy Rheese didn't smoke. Why did she need a cigarette lighter? I asked myself. I pressed the indentation and a blade flew open. The gadget *was* a functioning lighter—and a knife too. Its serrated blade could as easily peel an orange as cut a throat, I thought.

The gun and knife were small and easily overlooked. They had probably skipped Missy Rheese's mind on this busy first day of her new life in Brooks Hall, the Barnard College dormitory.

My eyes returned to the gun. Engravings on the stock identified it as being of .40 caliber and made by Tanfoglio. A stylish, Italian gun, I thought, though not one that I would enjoy shooting.

My best friend, Erika, is a gun nut. She enjoys shooting high powered weapons. This activity began after her mother and sister were raped and murdered.

Despite this, Erika and her father are as normal as people who have endured such horror can be. Erika plans to marry a wonderful boy, Clarence, and her father dates.

But he assures Erika that he won't get married—at least not before she does.

Erika's billionaire father maintains bodyguards for her safety, and insisted that she be trained in self-defense. Erika practices weekly at Greenwich's shooting range and frequently drags me along. She always chooses a high powered weapon but I prefer a .22 caliber pistol, one creating small blast and little recoil.

I caressed Missy Rheese's pistol. Though small, it felt heavy in my hand. Why did she feel the need for a pistol and particularly one of .40 caliber?

I didn't know Missy Rheese. We had been roommates for mere hours. I hadn't wanted to live on campus but traveling from my home in Connecticut to Barnard isn't easy. I need first take the Metro-North train from Greenwich to Grand Central Station. There, I must transfer to the subway and take the 42nd Street Shuttle to the 7th Avenue subway line which I take to the 116th Street station. After that comes a short walk.

This isn't a bad commute and many people have worse. But on some days my classes stretched until 9:00PM and this was bad. I would return to Greenwich after 11PM and need someone to pick me up at the station. I discussed this with my parents before school began.

"Commuting won't work," my father said, and my mother nodded agreement.

I agreed too but not happily. Apart from summer vacations or brief trips, I had never been away from home. Nearly everyone that I loved was in Greenwich. This included my boyfriend, Randy, who had just begun college at Yale.

The issue wasn't the cost of living in a dormitory since I had been awarded a full tuition scholarship including housing. It was my unease at being away from home, and maybe of growing up too. Perhaps that was why I had forgotten to bring such necessities as tampons.

After taking several of Missy Rheese's tampons, I replaced the pistol in the tampon box and re-covered it with her underwear. Then, after a thought, I retrieved the gun and wiped my fingerprints from it with a tissue.

Though my mother considers me reckless, my father knows that I am cautious. The gun laws in New York City are severe and I knew that it was nearly impossible to get a permit for a pistol. Who was my roommate? What have I gotten myself into by rooming with her? I asked myself.

Chapter 2

Guns might be bought for shooting at clay pigeons and paper targets. Knives have several uses too. But Missy Rheese's gun and switchblade were made to kill.

Yet she and her parents had seemed so sweet. They took me out for lunch after my parents left. My father is disabled by Lyme disease and my mother makes sure that he doesn't over-exert himself. They returned home soon after I was settled in my room.

Missy Rheese had already arrived. My first thought was that we could not be more different. I'm tall, red-haired, and was dressed in shirt and jeans. She is blond, petite, and wore a stylish sequined bodice and full skirt.

My clothing, apart from sneakers, had been bought at the Salvation Army Store in Port Jervis, New York which is close to Greenwich.

At Barnard, I would again be a poor girl amongst the wealthy. Though my father is a lawyer, his illness makes him unable to work. Our family survives on Social Security Disability payments, Food Stamps, and food from grateful local farmers who were my father's former clients. To no longer need explain my run-down clothes, I had long thought that I should get a tattoo: "Another Poor Girl."

Missy Rheese's Southern accent and elegant clothes created a puzzle. Why had we been placed as roommates since we appeared so different? I learned the probable reasons later that day.

Soon after arriving, Missy Rheese took her parents on a tour of the dormitory, to meet the First Year Focus Director and be assured of student safety. When they returned, she invited me to lunch with her parents. I hesitated but her parents insisted. They had probably wanted to get to know me better too.

There had been widely publicized cases of murder by roommates in New York City. They might have been concerned whether their daughter was safe with someone who looked so different. Or their invitation could have reflected simple courtesy.

Missy Rheese's parents were dressed in the expensively casual style of Greenwich. This made me feel like a relative of their household staff, perhaps their cook's daughter. This isn't how they treated me but I often get this feeling. Living an underprivileged life isn't easy.

I chatted with Missy Rheese as we walked to the garage that held her parents' car.

"Call me Missy," she said, with an engaging smile.

"I wondered about your name," I said.

"Having two first names is an old Southern custom. My brothers are Odis Lee, Quinton Lee, and William David though everyone uses only their first name."

I smiled but said nothing. Every place has its native customs. I remembered the food that I had to endure during my summer in London: baked beans for breakfast, if you can believe it.

I tried not to show my anxiety about dining with them. It's easier eating with friends and relatives who know that you're vegetarian. I feared that learning this, and that I was Mormon, would destroy the chance of Missy becoming the nearby, close friend that I needed.

"What are your brothers like?" I asked, turning our conversation to a topic that I hoped would be neutral.

"*Terrible!* What are brothers like?" Missy replied, with a laugh.

"*Missy Rheese!*" her mother called from a few steps ahead.

"I wouldn't know. I have three sisters," I said, volunteering an innocent fact.

"Well, maybe not *really* terrible. You'd love Quinton. He's nineteen and very good looking. He attends Dartmouth and wants to be a lawyer," Missy said.

Hmm, I thought, here's a point of similarity.

"My father is a lawyer," I said, stating one of my positive features.

I could have added that he was really my adoptive father, that my biological father lived in London and had been a spy for Britain's Secret Intelligence Service, and that my "courtesy father," Vladimir, is a former Russian general who manages a security company in Germany.

Obviously, I didn't say these things. I wanted Missy and her parents to consider me simple and uninteresting.

We settled in the car. It was a Mercedes SUV. Erika's father also owns one but his car is armored.

"I'm a lawyer too. What's your father's specialty," Missy's father asked, from the front seat, as he slowed abruptly to avoid an aggressively driven taxi. "They don't drive like this in Charleston," he said, shaking his head.

"My parents try to avoid driving in the City," I said sympathetically, before answering his question and affirming my pedigree. "Greenwich is a small town. Our family's roots go back to the 19th century. An ancestor was a Chief Justice of the Connecticut Supreme Court. My dad does some criminal and family work but his major interest is maritime law."

Missy's father nodded his approval.

"The restaurant we're going to is special," he said.

CHAPTER 3

Per Se is on the 4th floor of the Time Warner Center at 60th Street and Columbus Circle. That I had never heard of it is no surprise. My family no longer eats out. Things were different before we entered the poverty class. Restaurants don't take food stamps.

Missy's parents led the way. At the building, we took the elevator to the 4th floor. The restaurant's entrance lay to the left of a decorative blue door.

"*Zagat* rated Per Se as the best restaurant in New York City," Missy's father said, as the waiter led us to our table.

Per Se isn't large. It's a cozy place for small gatherings of well-off people. There were two fixed-cost, nine-course options for dinner and each cost $310. This didn't include such extras as foie gras, truffles, or an alcoholic drink if that was your pleasure.

We were given two menus: a Tasting of Vegetables menu and a Chef's Tasting menu. I relaxed when I saw them. Now I won't have to apologize for being vegetarian, I thought.

"We chose this restaurant because Missy is vegetarian," her mother said.

"So am I," I confessed, giving Missy a big smile.

Could this be why we had been placed together as roommates? I wondered, before receiving another surprise.

Missy's father refused the waiter's offer of the wine menu.

"My family is Mormon. We don't drink alcohol or tea or coffee. Mineral water will be fine for us."

Missy looked uncomfortable but I relaxed even more. Apart from religion and diet, I was like every other girl. At least most of the time if you don't ask my mother.

"My family is Mormon too," I volunteered, and the table erupted in smiles. It was like when you meet a classmate from years before whether you had liked them or not.

Having established what one might consider to be the old school tie, Missy's parents introduced themselves to me as Dixon and Annalyn ("call me Annie").

"What's Greenwich like," Annie asked. "We've heard so much about it."

I looked blank. For me, Greenwich is home and a typical small town–if you ignore the large number of millionaires and that Erika's father is a multi-billionaire.

"It's like any small town with one main street. Along Greenwich Avenue are restaurants and stores including an Apple store. There are two beaches that are reached by town ferry.

"It's growing fast. Hedge funds are opening offices since many of their executives live there. Metro-North runs trains regularly and you can reach Manhattan in under an hour. This adds to the town's appeal."

I had spoken in a rush. I wanted to satisfy their curiosity but also not to reveal the painful facts of my life.

The Tasting of Vegetables that Missy and I chose was...vegetables, no matter how you slice them, to make one of my bad puns. It began with Watercress Veloute which consisted of rhubarb, garlic, and horseradish sauce. Then came Turnip and Cashew Tofu; a tasty combination of avocado, radishes, mandarins; and what was called Ruby Beet Emulsion.

These dishes were followed by Charred Eggplant Barbajuan, Swiss Card Subric, Degustation De Pommes De Terre, Per Se Ricotta Agnolotti, Vulto Cremery's Miranda, and Jasper Hill Farm's Bayley Hazen Blue. I won't bore you with their ingredients.

The dessert portion of the meal was a drawn-out affair with a choice of donuts, mini ice-cream sandwiches, macaroons, and more. There was a cake to celebrate Missy's birthday though it wouldn't be for many months.

"Missy will be busy in school and Dixon will be overwhelmed with his duties," Annie explained.

I gave a blank look.

"Dixon was just appointed bishop," she said, with pride.

I immediately understood. A Mormon bishop serves without pay for four to seven years and his position is demanding. He conducts worship services and introduces the speakers at meetings, often adding a few words.

Church members seek guidance from the bishop. He listens to their confessions for serious sins and helps them through their repentance process. He also oversees the payment of tithes and offerings in his ward (geographic unit), is responsible for its finances, and helps church members who come on hard times by supplying them with food and household goods from the Bishop's Storehouse.

In short, the bishop is a very busy man for he must carry out these duties while working at his job and maintaining his own family. Necessarily, his wife helps with his duties and she becomes very busy too.

Dixon turned toward me.

"How is your participation in Personal Progress going?" he asked, in a kindly tone.

I hoped that my gulp wasn't noticeable as I tried to think of an agreeable response. I was not the conventional Mormon girl that Dixon apparently considered me. No Mormon bishop would consider me that.

Personal Progress is the Mormon achievement program for teenage girls. They are expected to set goals in eight value areas: faith, divine nature, individual worth, knowledge, choice and accountability, good works, integrity, and virtue.

While my family attends church every Sunday and is respected, we are not rigidly religious. I do attend the teenage girl's discussion group each Sunday, but also the monthly chat group of Greenwich Babysitters Registry LLC, the business that Erika and I began. There, we discuss both babysitting and dating. Recent topics have included how much sex is too much in a relationship and oral sex. The Mormon group talks over different things. You get the idea.

Moreover Randy, the boy that I plan to marry, isn't Mormon or religious, and Erika's Christmas and Easter services consist of brunches at L'Escale. That's an expensive French restaurant on Greenwich's Steamboat Road.

What should I tell Dixon? I asked myself. Certainly not the facts.

"I do my best but I'm a work in progress," I replied, finally.

"As are we all, for all our lives," Dixon said, giving me a warm smile and a fatherly pat on the hand.

The rest of the evening was uneventful. Missy and I were back in the dormitory at a little after nine.

I hadn't raised the issue of her gun and knife since I didn't know what to do. While pistols are common in some states, this isn't true in New York City. My informing a Residence Advisor could get Missy expelled or arrested and I didn't want either to happen. I liked her and her parents, and the last thing that the church needed was a scandal.

I didn't know what to do and began chattering. I hoped to learn more about her and for this issue to come up naturally.

"Thanks for the tampons. I don't know how I could have forgotten them," I said.

"It happens," Missy said, without looking up from her iPad as she checked her Facebook page.

I spoke again after a moment.

"I have three sisters. I can't imagine what growing up with three brothers would have been like."

Missy stiffened before staring at me.

"I grew up with two brothers," she said.

Am I losing it? I asked myself. I'm sure she said that she had three brothers. If this brain lapse is her's—if she's this scattered—there's no question what I must do regardless of the consequences.

I persisted. Maybe I hadn't heard her correctly. Perhaps one of the brothers is a courtesy brother as Vladimir is my courtesy father. I remembered their names.

"Didn't you say that you had three brothers: Odis Lee, Quinton Lee, and William David?" I asked, in a puzzled tone.

Missy's eyes watered. She didn't speak for a long time. I waited silently.

"Everyone says that I won't face the truth. Odis disappeared ten years ago and no one but me believes him alive."

Chapter 4

It's rude to stare at a troubled person but I couldn't help it. Things were becoming too weird. First, this picture-perfectly dressed girl with an engaging Southern accent and a Mormon bishop for a father carries a pistol and switchblade. Then there's her story of a vanished brother who only she considers to be alive. It didn't make sense.

I instinctively moved farther away from her, and removed myself psychologically too. I began studying her rather than relating to her as a friend and Missy sensed this.

"You don't have to worry, I'm not crazy though I sometimes wish that I were. Then I could see a shrink or take pills and things would change."

Though still staring, my feelings began to change. None of us is as sane as we pretend, I thought, as I remembered some events in my life. I hate horror movies because I have lived them.

Every person is created to be a mystery to every other. Everyone has their own *Great War* and maybe what happened to Odis was Missy's. People are advised to stay out of another's business but our behavior with our friends defines who we are. That–and fate–place us on the paths we follow.

I have always told myself that fear is like a wall with the view improving as you climb it. I sat beside Missy and approached her wall.

"Tell me about it," I said.

"OK, but not now. I need sleep. In the morning during breakfast."

Missy left her bed to plug in her iPad and phone. Having done this, and without another word, she returned to bed. I understood when she covered her head with the comforter. I had slept like that when I had nightmares.

Brooks Hall was built over a hundred years ago. The newer residences are for upper class students. First Year students must live at "the Hall," as students call it. The Student Health Center is located on the lower level.

Living at Brooks is like living in a motel except that there is a shared bathroom on each floor instead of a private bathroom and there is no air-conditioning.
The wireless Internet is free but there is no cable TV unless you are willing to pay for it. A TV lounge is on the first floor.

The list of prohibited items is long and include air conditioners, double-sided tape for hanging posters, pets (except for a small fish tank), candles, more furniture or halogen lamps, a hot plate or toaster oven or microwave, a heater, and some things that I would never consider bringing like a water bed, a hookah, or drugs.

Some of these things, as a microwave, are permitted in a suite kitchen. Guns and knives aren't permitted anywhere.

Our room was one of the larger doubles, being ten by twenty feet according to the housing brochure. It lay at one end of the corridor, the communal bathroom was in the middle of the corridor, and the laundry room was at the other end. Our room held twin beds, two desks and chairs, two dressers, and closets. The furniture was modern, and workers handled the cleaning.

As First Year Students we had to participate in the Platinum Meal Plan. This consisted of nineteen meals a week, taken cafeteria style. Thankfully, the food included vegetarian and vegan options.

The cafeteria was located in a neighboring building that connected to ours through a tunnel. Ten hours later, Missy and I passed through that tunnel for breakfast–and for her explanation of Odis' disappearance.

CHAPTER 5

We were silent while walking to the dining hall, ignoring the affectionate couplings about us. Our dormitory was coed. It was a rousing arrangement for most of the students though probably few of them were virgin.

Sexual activity isn't undertaken lightly by Mormons. The condoms that Erika had purchased for me remained unused. Did Missy hold my attitude or, Mormon or not, were Southern girls more easy-going? I didn't know and didn't care so long as she didn't invite a boy to a sleepover in our room. What worried me were her weapons.

If she couldn't reassure me about her sanity–why she felt the need for a gun and a switchblade–I had already decided what I would do. I would hide the weapons, say that I was having a panic attack, and ask her to accompany me to the Health Center. When alone with a doctor, I would reveal that my real anxiety was about Missy.

We chose nearly the same food. It had been my habitual breakfast in high school: orange juice, a whole-wheat bagel, the most nutritious cereal being offered, a banana, and milk. I had suggested to the cook that soy burgers be available but this never happened. Only a handful of students had come for this early (free) meal and I was the only vegetarian.

Margaret of Greenwich

I steered us toward a corner table, one far from the other students though the cafeteria was only half full. Despite the meal plan being required for First Year students, most either slept late or ate in a local restaurant. I chewed my bagel and waited silently until Missy spoke.

"You probably think that I'm crazy," she said.

I said nothing. Let a story be told in its own way, I told myself, echoing the advice that my lawyer-father had given me.

"Why would I believe Odis to be alive when everyone is sure that he's dead?" Missy asked, rhetorically.

I remained silent. Let Missy stay on her roll, my father seemed to tell me.

"What would convince you that someone is alive?" Missy asked.

I didn't know how to reply. Did she mean *medically alive*? I did my best.

"They have brain and heart activity without external help," I replied.

"That's a good answer but it's not the one that I was looking for. You're smart. Would I ask you such a basic question?" Missy said, forcefully taking charge of our conversation.

I shook my head.

"Let me tell you about Odis. When you know him as well as I do and what's been happening, you too will be convinced that no matter how many people believe him dead, *he must be alive!*"

Chapter 6

Missy's eyes became unfocused as she looked off into the distance. Because she seemed to be having a hard time getting started, I asked the most non-threatening questions that I could think of.

"How old is Odis? What does he look like? What is he like?"

My questions had their desired effect. Missy's face brightened and she looked directly at me.

"Oh, you'd love him. He's twenty-nine and tall and good looking. He's blond like me but his eyes are a deeper shade of blue, and he's really smart.

"He loves fishing. When he was fourteen he invented a lure with a tiny battery that flashed a blood-red light down its tail when it moved through the water. Fish think that it's an injured prey and strike. When his invention was compared to top-selling American lures, fishermen using his lure caught three times as many fish. Stores picked them up and thousands were sold!"

Missy was speaking in a rush. She was on another roll and I feared interrupting her. I stared at Missy with a broad smile plastered to my face.

But talking about Odis took a toll and she shut down again. She began eating her oatmeal, one dainty spoonful at a time, while staring into the bowl. I waited for a minute before asking a direct question, one that would tell me something important.

"Missy, Odis sounds lovely and if I didn't have a boyfriend I'd pester you to introduce us. But what happened to him? Where is he now?"

Missy's hand froze in mid-air as I spoke. After carefully placing her spoon in the bowl, she looked up.

"No one knows. He was a freshman at Harvard, a computer science major. My parents drove him to Boston and he phoned a week later to say that he loved school. Things were different by Christmas.

"My parents didn't notice the change but I did. He had always looked at me in a special way. I'm the only girl in the family and being my oldest brother he had always been protective. I didn't need protecting but I liked it. Now he ignored me. He was guarded and looked frightened. Six weeks later he vanished, and so completely that it was as if he had never existed.

"The school was in an uproar. Harvard students do not simply disappear. If they drop out it's to start a billion dollar company. Didn't you hear about Odis? It was a big story."

I shook my head. Each year since I could remember a new upheaval had entered my life. On some days I didn't notice the sky.

"The police couldn't find a trace of him, nor could a private investigator that my father had hired. Everyone believes that he's dead but I'm sure he's not!"

"Why?" I asked. It was the only logical question.

Missy swallowed hard before speaking.

"Well, Odis and I had a tradition. Each birthday he gave me the same Pandora charm. He told me it meant that he would always love me and be there for me. This custom began on my fifth birthday and he had given me five charms before he disappeared. I wear this necklace every day."

Missy unfastened the necklace and handed it to me. It held only Pandora Heart Silver Dangle charms inscribed with the words "YOU AND ME." I had bought it for my baby sister the previous year.

I counted the charms. There were fourteen of them.

"It's beautiful. You've continued buying them," I said.

"You don't understand! They never stopped coming," Missy said, in an agitated tone.

"*What?*"

"On each birthday I receive the same charm, mailed from a different city. Odis is sending them to assure me that he loves me. *This* is why I'm sure that he's alive."

Chapter 7

"That is *some* story," I said slowly, and Missy nodded.

"What do your parents say?" I asked.

"That the charms are being sent by an admirer," Missy replied, waving her hand in a depreciative manner. "That many people know me and any of them might be sending it. They can't deal with his disappearance. They want to forget but I never will. He *is* alive and I'll find him no matter what it takes. I'll go to the brink for him–and beyond. We're bound together in this life and the next."

I understood. Mormons believe that families are knotted together throughout eternity. This, though with some families, members can barely tolerate each other.

When I touched her hand to comfort her, the thought of her gun and knife re-entered my mind. Was she carrying them? I wondered. I nodded absent-mindedly.

"Good. I knew that we would be friends from the moment we met. I'm counting on you to help me," Missy said, and a smile brightened her face.

My simple nod had involved me.

Missy looked toward the clock.

"We have Orientation. Are you finished?" she asked.

Margaret of Greenwich

I wrapped the remainder of my bagel in a napkin and placed it in my backpack. She was right. It wouldn't be good to be late for the New Student Orientation Program (NSOP) though nothing that I learned there could calm my raging thoughts. School had fallen away from my list of worries.

The NSOP was ten times worse than I expected though that is understandable. Put hundreds of teenagers from all over the world in one group and you won't get more than a semblance of unity. But the Barnard officials tried.

They had put together a week of talks about "living skills" with the goal of keeping us safe. From exactly what I wasn't sure but certainly from what had occurred with Odis.

The reality is that unpleasant things happen in Manhattan and elsewhere. There are fires and car accidents and drug overdoses and murders. You will meet helpful people when you are lost and those who will try to take advantage of you.

For some, girl-school Barnard was lesbian heaven. For the others, there were hundreds of boys attending Columbia College across the street. Older, friendly students warned us about horny teachers.

I had been to Manhattan many times with school classes, my parents, and friends. I had ridden the subway, ignored panhandlers, gawked at skyscrapers, and bought frozen yoghurt in Greenwich Village. I had been to the Statue of Liberty and the Empire State Building. When my dad still worked, we had shopped at Macy's. But for most of the First Year girls these experiences were new.

During that week, Missy clung to me as if were joined at the hip. This might have been because we now shared the same goal: to find Odis and lift the darkness enveloping her family. Attending classes was something that we would do along the way. By taking the same classes we could work together and complete the assignments in half the time.

It was while relaxing in our room after an exhausting day of Freshman Orientation that I finally asked *my* key question.

"Missy, why do you need a gun and a switchblade?"

Chapter 8

"I wondered when you'd bring it up. I was never good at hiding things," Missy replied, with more annoyance than anger.

"I didn't mean to pry but I couldn't help seeing them when I was looking for a tampon. They were in the box," I said.

"Not too smart, huh?"

"Hiding things well takes practice. It took me hours to find my dad's love letter but he was a spy and expert at such things," I said, sympathetically.

"We both have secrets," Missy said, with widening eyes. "No, I don't plan to kill anyone. They're for self-defense."

"Defense against who?"

"I don't know, we don't know. My father gave me the gun and my uncle taught me to shoot. I bought the knife online."

"Do you have a permit for the gun?" I asked, gingerly.

Considering what I had done throughout my life, I'm about the last person to let a law stop me from doing what I believe is necessary. But New York City has the toughest gun laws in the nation. Even forgetful people with permits from other states have been arrested. The image of genteel Missy being imprisoned at Rikers

Island, a jail known for its brutality, caused me to shudder and Missy noticed.

"What?" she asked.

"I imagined you being in jail. I don't want another roommate."

"You won't be getting one. I have a permit for the gun," Missy said.

Getting a permit to carry a pistol in New York City is a little less difficult than winning the state's lottery but not by much. One of my dad's friends had shared this problem and he was a diamond merchant who really needed a gun. "It depends on who you know," he had said.

"How did you manage to get the permit?" I asked, with real interest.

Missy gave me the same answer that my dad got.

"It depends on who you know. My father's law school friend is in Congress and my uncle is the SAC, Special Agent-in-Charge, of Manhattan's FBI office."

"OK, but why do you feel the need for a gun in the safest big city in American?" I asked.

"Boston is safe and look what happened to Odis. My parents worry and are doing what they can to protect me. Maybe the gun isn't needed and I know that it's on the school's prohibited list but..."

"A gun is like toilet paper. When you need it, you need it bad," I said.

"Huh?"

"A friend who was in the German Special Forces said that," I explained.

I waved my hand to indicate that I didn't want to explain and she changed the subject.

"You're not afraid of guns, are you?" she asked.

"No."

"Have you shot a pistol?"

"I had lessons but be careful how you carry it. There are always accidents."

"Trust me, I know what I'm doing," Missy said.

That day I did though what she said turned into the understatement of the year.

Chapter 9

My lawyer-father once told me that you shouldn't push a person to talk about something until they're ready. If you do, you won't get the whole, true story and that's what counts.

So I didn't push Missy. She showed me the "safety" pocket holster that she owned, described the operation of the pistol, and promised that she wouldn't draw it unless we were threatened. Then we dropped the subject.

I know about guns and realized that her uncle had done a good job of training her. I also knew that Missy wasn't dumb. She understood that if Barnard learned of her gun she would be expelled. Smoking pot in the dorm might be tolerated but not having a pistol in gun-fearing New York City, whether she was legally permitted to or not.

The mystery concerning Odis receded to the background of our thinking as classes approached. Everyone's attention, whether they were straight or gay, perked up during one introductory lecture.

It was dating advice given by a math professor. This sounded strange even to us but its real purpose was to encourage girls to major in math.

None of the more than one hundred girls in the room whispered or slurped their soda as Professor Creighton spoke. She held our rapt attention.

Margaret of Greenwich

Professor Creighton said that math isn't mysterious but is the study of patterns, like how the weather changes and cities grow. She said that life is full of patterns and among these are love: from the number of sexual partners that we have during our life to who we choose on an Internet dating site, and more.

Professor Creighton said that mathematics grew in importance because it is the basis on which every modern achievement rests. Then, returning to the topic that had perked the interest of all in the room, she asked a rhetorical question: How can you find your ideal mate?

Professor Creighton said that several years ago a single mathematician had calculated that there were more intelligent extraterrestrial civilizations than eligible men for her by using the Drake equation. She said that she won't bother explaining this equation since we could learn about it in her course. "It always contains more Columbia boys than girls and thus includes a dating component too," she added, with a smile.

At this comment, the room burst into the first laughter that had occurred in any of the Freshmen Orientation lectures. This teacher certainly knows how to win her audience, I thought. I would take her class.

Professor Creighton said that when you begin dating you should not choose the first potential mate since you are inexperienced and don't yet know who is available. If you want to settle down by the time you are forty, mathematics says that you should reject thirty-seven percent of your dates until just after your twenty-fourth birthday, and then pick the next person that comes along who is better than everyone you have met before. "This will give you the best possible chance of finding the love-of-your-life."

Professor Creighton's next advice, about relationships, was equally surprising. She said that the most successful couples have a "dynamic interaction." Rather than ignoring tiny disagreements, they resolve them quickly so that feelings don't get bottled up and little things are blown out of proportion. Thus, "having frequent arguments in a relationship is good, having rare arguments is dangerous."

"Now, how many of you will consider taking my class?" Professor Creighton asked, with a big smile, as she concluded her lecture.

Everyone raised their hand and she was given a standing ovation!

Chapter 10

I'm not a sociable person though those who know me casually would dispute this. I have a few best friends and one, Erika, considers me her sister. But while other girls have Facebook friends numbering in the hundreds or even thousands, mine remain in the very low double digits. This consists of my real friends, the teenage employees of the Greenwich babysitting business that Erika and I owned and managed, and the girls from the Greenwich Mormon Church's teen discussion group.

Missy is like me though she had not always been. She said that she changed after Odis disappeared. Pain, whether from injury or illness or loss, does that to you, I thought.

So apart from attending the required First Year Student Orientation outings and lectures, Missy and I stayed to ourselves. When others spontaneously joined us in the cafeteria, they would quickly sense our nature and not return. We weren't unfriendly but not seeking friends.

Two days before classes began, our conversation returned to Odis. We were sitting on a bench in front of the Columbia University library, watching the hurrying students in the quadrangle. Earlier, we had walked down Broadway to 72nd Street before returning by bus. Riding a bus or subway holds charm for those brought up in car dependent towns.

We had been talking the usual, our impressions of Barnard and girls in the dormitory, when Missy suddenly changed the subject.

"Will you help me to find Odis?" she asked, uncertainly.

Missy wanted to firm up my earlier hint of aid, to make certain that Odis' disappearance had become my priority too.

I understood where she was coming from. Because people can't tolerate unending doubt, they make up the best possible story and live as if it were true. Was it possible that Missy was correct and Odis lived? Yes, I told myself. And it was equally possible that he was dead–as everyone else believed–no matter how many charms Missy received.

Still, Missy had become my friend and you don't desert a friend. I knew that her painful search would continue whether I joined it or not.

After several moments of silence, I repeated the learned advice of Sherlock Holmes in *The Adventure of the Red-Headed League*: "The more bizarre a thing is, the less mysterious it proves to be."

Missy gripped my hand tightly. We both knew that my answer had been a definite "yes."

Chapter 11

The Brooks Hall Focus Director had scheduled a round of social activities for the First Year residents living there. These were held in the TV lounge on the first floor. Her likely intention was to keep us out of the local bars. Boys from Columbia College were invited and the girls were ready, dressed or barely clad depending on their fashion style.

Missy and watched as we slipped out of the building. Unlike them, we were casually dressed in shirt, jeans, and sneakers. Plastic bags from Macy's held our phones and other necessities. Missy's pistol lay in her holster, and her switchblade was in my pocket.

Though being committed to the idea that Odis was alive and needed our help, we couldn't be sure. Every person is a mystery to every other.

To avoid being seen by a Residence Advisor, we looked for an out-of-the way place to huddle, a restaurant where no self-respecting preppie would want to be seen. We found it, nine blocks south of campus and off Broadway.

The restaurant advertised itself as being Cuban-American. That it was three-quarters full meant that the food was good. It also looked clean. The menu was posted in the window but we had never eaten any of the dishes on it. Still, New York City has a good health department so nothing bad can happen, I told myself. That proved to be true though these can also be one's last words.

No one in the restaurant looked like a student and it was so noisy that we couldn't be overheard. The men looked poor but normal. Three girls in their early twenties sat by the window. They wore micro skirts and exaggerated makeup.

"They're hookers," I whispered to Missy, as we walked to a table in the rear.

The girls had eyed us suspiciously when we entered but then ignored us. They decided we weren't competition. That's the kind of place it was.

The waiter dropped two menus on the table and waited. We planned to be talking for a long time and ordering only juice wouldn't cut it. I picked up the menu hesitantly.

""I'm hungry," Missy said, reaching for her menu and interrupting my thinking.

I was hungry too but also broke. My family is poor and my scholarship didn't cover eating out. I intended to find a part-time job to get spending money.

"Order a lot, we'll be here for a while. I'm paying!" Missy insisted.

"Thank you," I said softly.

I had earlier told Missy of my father's disability and my family's financial problems.

Despite being vegetarian, ordering wasn't difficult since we do eat fish and milk products. Still, our choices were limited and we wound up choosing mostly the same

42

dishes: Camarones Al Ajillo (sautéed garlic shrimp), Ensalada De Cuba (a mixed green salad with tomatoes, avocado, red onions, and a balsamic/vinaigrette dressing), a side dish of Moros (black beans mixed with white rice), and Salmon (pan-seared salmon with coconut rice, shrimp, and lobster sauce).

For dessert I chose Bon Bon Cubano (a flourless chocolate cake with a molten core, strawberries, vanilla ice cream, and coconut) and Missy chose Tres Leches De Lima (vanilla sponge cake, key lime curd, cream, kiwi strawberry salsa, and macadamia tuile). We drank bottled water.

The waiter smiled appreciably at our orders.

"All this food will go to my hips," Missy remarked, after he left.

"We can skip breakfast tomorrow," I said, reassuringly.

"Where do we start?" Missy asked.

She had instinctively appointed me boss. This probably happened when I told her that my biological father had been a British spy. I didn't say that that there are no genes for that kind of work. Judging by my life, I only half believed it.

Chapter 12

The food was good and eating gave me time to think since I was clueless what to do. How do you search for someone that everyone believes is dead—except for his sister who may be no saner than you? On some days, my mother isn't too sure about my mind.

I chewed, drank, and considered. A good first step would be to know the kind of man that Odis was. I still knew nothing about him except that he was smart and inventive and had been studying computer science at Harvard when he disappeared.

People think differently. My best friend, Erika, seems able to jump logic and arrive at the correct solution by instinct. At this point she might already have solved our mystery. But I think more slowly and have to worry about logic. This reinforced my feeling that we needed to understand Odis better. Which is what I said.

"Missy, to figure out what happened we have to know Odis better. All I know is the little that you've told me. What was he like? What were his friends like? Who didn't he like? Did he have a girlfriend? What did he want to do with his life? Did he plan to go on a mission?"

A *mission* is the missionary work that many Mormon youth undertake though fewer now than in the past. Still, Missy's family was far more religious than mine.

"I don't like to talk about him," Missy said, and her eyes watered.

"I know it's hard but if we're to find him..." I insisted.

"I don't know all that much except that I loved—love—him."

I nodded my understanding.

"I was nine when he vanished. Some things, like his girlfriend, he wouldn't talk about with me since he was so much older. What I have are vague memories from what my parents and brothers said. They talked about him for years."

Again, I nodded my understanding. "Never interrupt when a client is telling their story," is what my dad advised beginning lawyers in his office, and I continued following his advice.

"What I best remember is his good heart. He was always willing to help another person even if it meant taking heat.

"A boy who walked funny was being bullied outside school. First, it was just with words but one day they frightened him with a knife and pushed and slapped him.

"Odis didn't know the boy but he stood up for him and became a legend in school. The bully slashed at Odis with his knife. He managed to cut his arm before Odis smashed the knife from his hand with his hockey stick and sent the others running. Every day after that, Odis ate lunch with the boy and walked him home."

"He sounds like quite a guy, risking his life for a stranger," I said, slowly. "I can see why losing him would mean emptiness beyond belief."

"Not only for me. After walking the boy home, his sister bandaged Odis' arm. They became engaged just before he vanished."

Chapter 13

I played with my food to give me time to think. I ate the chocolate cake slowly and dawdled over the bottled water. The problem was that I had no idea where to begin.

A year before, during my summer in London, I had tried to learn about my biological father that I had never known. I questioned my grandmother and others who knew him. I studied his favorite books and videos, and discovered his unfinished love letter to my biological mother. That task was a cakewalk compared to this.

Missy was young when Odis vanished. How much did she know about her brother? How accurate was the gossip that she overheard? Good theories derive from good facts and Missy was giving me few of these. My face revealed how discouraged I felt.

"I ask only that you do your best," Missy said, placing her hand over mine.

"I will! Do you have anything personal of his that exposes his thinking? His ex-girlfriend might have letters," I suggested.

"The last that I heard she was married and living in Wyoming. My parents haven't had contact with her since Odis disappeared. She wouldn't welcome contact and being reminded."

I felt hopeless and looked down at my plate.

"But I do have Odis' diary," Missy said.

"What? Where is it?" I exclaimed, so loudly that people at nearby tables stared.

"The detective took his newest computer but Odis also had an old one that he kept a diary on it. I didn't tell the detective about it. I didn't want to lose something of Odis. It might have been childish but...

"Odis taught me to use a computer because he started using them when he was young. My parents and other brothers were computer illiterates. With my dad working long hours and Odis being so much older, I guess that he sometimes saw himself as being my father."

Missy's eyes watered, and I nodded.

I felt excited and immediately lost interest in the best chocolate cake that I had ever eaten.

"Let's get going. I want to see Odis' files," I said.

"OK, but there's a problem. I tried reading his diary but couldn't because it's password protected."

"That's OK. My boyfriend is a hacker genius," I said, confidently.

I hoped that he wouldn't let us down.

Chapter 14

As luck would have it, upon leaving the restaurant we nearly collided with the Brooks Hall First-Year Focus Director. She fixed us with the suspicious look of mothers who *know* that their child did something wrong.

"Why aren't you at the Residence social?" she asked, giving us a hard stare.

You don't really want to know, I thought, but of course didn't say. Before Missy could blurt the truth, I spoke up–and so forcefully that Missy was sure to get the point.

"It's Missy's birthday and I wanted to take her someplace special. She *loves* Spanish food," I piped up, in my most innocent tone.

"That's *just* what we like to see, roommates becoming lifelong friends. Happy birthday, Missy," the Director said.

A smile lit her face as she walked off. She had been holding hands with a man wearing a wedding ring. Her hand was ring free, and they walked away quickly.

"That was quick thinking. You're a persuasive liar," Missy said, a bit warily, when they were half-way down the street.

"I've had practice," I said dryly, before adding, "But it was always for a good reason."

We walked silently for a block before Missy spoke.

"What's your boyfriend like?" she asked.

I took Randy's photo from my wallet.

"He's good looking," she said, after several moments of study.

"Yes, and he's also very smart and dependable and doesn't play around."

"How long have you been going together?"

"I've known him since grade school. We became a couple when we were thirteen and plan to marry after college," I said.

"*Thirteen*?" Missy asked, with surprise.

According to Mormon custom, teenagers shouldn't begin dating, and then only as a group, until they're sixteen, and not date exclusively until they've graduated high school or completed their religious mission. That's the official teaching but how many follow these practices today is questionable. Still, Missy's father is a Mormon bishop so...

"What did your parents think?" Missy asked.

"I never asked them and they never said. They trust their kids. My mom's the nervous type and my dad's a lawyer so he knows what not to ask," I said.

We walked on for another block in silence.

"I wish my parents were like that," Missy said.

At the dormitory, we became quickly surrounded by partying students. Some looked happy and others were trying to. It was like a typical high school gym party.

After our minimum expressions of giggles, laughter, and silliness, we got to our room. There, Missy took her brother's laptop from a suitcase. It was an old Dell running Windows XP.

"He souped it up but my smartphone is more powerful," Missy said, as she turned on the machine.

The familiar Windows log-in screen came up, Missy entered her password, and I took over her desk chair.

"Is there anything of yours that I shouldn't look at?" I asked.

"No. I keep the porn and my nudes on another machine," Missy replied with a grin, which I returned.

"OK. Which files came with the machine and which are yours?" I asked.

"Mine begin with 'missy,' the others are his. I saved his files onto a USB," she said, handing it to me.

"Do you have another copy?" I asked.

"No."

"I'll copy it onto my laptop and save it to my online storage too. We can't be too careful."

I scanned the names of Odis' files. None said "diary" and I looked up.

"It's spelled 'dairy,' he misspelled it," Missy said.

I found the file. As Missy had said, it required a password to open.

"I'll call Randy," I said.

"Where is he?"

"At Yale. He's a pre-med but will never be a doctor. He faints at the sight of blood."

"So why is he pre-med?"

"That's a whole other story," I said.

Then I sprawled out on my bed and explained.

Chapter 15

"Randy's father is a doctor and wants Randy to be one too. But Randy faints when he sees blood or gets an injection.

"To cure this, his father insisted that Randy be present at his sister's birth, 'to knock the craziness from him,' but it didn't. I caught Randy when he fainted. He wound up in a bed alongside his mother. It embarrassed everyone.

"Even this didn't change his dad's mind. Now he insists that Randy will outgrow his fear and it'll be gone by the time he begins medical school. Randy knows that it won't but since his father is paying for his college there's nothing that he can do except take as many classes in what he loves on the side. These are in math and computer science.

"We plan to marry after he graduates. He should be able to get a teaching fellowship while studying for his doctorate and I'll work too. Someday, Randy will be super successful and his father will come around. His sister can be the second doctor in the family."

"I'm jealous. You have your life all planned out," Missy said.

"Maybe. But like they say, man proposes and God disposes. What are your plans?"

"My only plan is to find Odis. I came north to Barnard to be closer to where he disappeared. My life feels as if it's been on hold since then."

"Do you have a boyfriend?"

"I can't. There's a hole in me and I couldn't relate to a boy."

Missy's matter-of-fact tone bothered me. It was as if she had given up on life.

"Don't give up. The best way to lengthen our days is to walk steadily with a purpose."

"Who said that?" Missy asked.

"Charles Dickens. He's my father's favorite author—the English dad who is a spy. My adoptive father is the lawyer."

"Do you always follow the law?" Missy asked, after several moments of silence.

"I try, but when things are going disastrous it's sometimes best to toss the rules. I'll phone Randy."

When speaking with Randy, I briefly stated my reason for calling. Not that I didn't want us to talk but that could be later.

"I need a favor," I said to Randy.

"Anything."

"My roommate, Missy, has a brother who went missing ten years ago. Everyone except her considers him dead."

I stopped speaking for a moment to let this fact sink in.

"OK," Randy said slowly.

"Since she was little, he had given her a Pandora Heart Silver Dangle charm every birthday. They never stopped coming."

*"*They never stopped coming!" Randy said. *"She still gets them?"*

"Yes."

"Did anyone else know their custom?"

I asked Missy.

"My parents and brothers knew but it wasn't something that I talked about. It would have seemed babyish," Missy said.

I shared this fact with Randy and told him why I had called.

"Missy has her brother's diary from his old computer. But the file is password protected and I want you to hack it," I said.

Chapter 16

"Do you believe her story?" Randy asked.

"I trust her judgment," I replied, indirectly.

I tried to sound more certain than I felt. Still, I sensed that Odis' disappearance wasn't a simple matter, if any of them ever are.

I doubted that Randy would refuse my appeal since they involved two loves: a hacking challenge, and me.

Randy does anything that I ask. He proved this in the past though having had misgivings at some of my requests. But despite the risks and our fears, everything had turned out OK. I hoped that our luck would continue.

Randy's reply was a question, "Is it a rush job?"

"Missy has been suffering for years," I answered, again indirectly.

"Send me the file. I'll make coffee and get busy,"

"How are your classes going?" I asked.

"I took exams to get out of the basic math and science classes and am doing independent study with a medical researcher. It's not bad at all."

"*Medical*?" I asked, with surprise, thinking of his terror of doctors' offices and continuing fear that he had caught some dreadful illness.

"There's no blood involved. I summarize research and will be thanked in his publication. My dad is very happy."

"Do you think you can be a doctor?" I asked.

"I told Wolfie–Wolfgang–my teacher of my fear of blood. He said it isn't unusual and that nervous medical students often become the most considerate doctors. He also said that much medical school study is now done on computers and not as gory as it was. But I doubt I'll wind up in medicine. I like working on my own too much."

"Whatever, but I want you taking care of yourself. Get enough sleep and eat well, my darling."

My darling had become my favorite term for him.

"Yes, mamma," he replied, though his tone was affectionate.

"Love you," I said softly, and he replied, "Always."

Using these words to end to our phone calls had become customary. We had begun thinking about the practices to institute in our marriage and decided on one. Each evening, Randy would hold me in his arms and we would share the events of that day. We would do this with each of our children too.

After I hung up, I shared this with Missy.

"I have vowed not to love until finding Odis," she said, with wet eyes.

Chapter 17

We could do nothing more until hearing from Randy. While waiting, we attended classes, listened to student complaints without commenting, and distracted ourselves with the organized chaos of student life.

Attending Barnard College was a refreshing change from our rule-filled high schools. After the first class of any of our courses, we could have stayed away and gone unnoticed. We didn't though the role-playing games debating women's rights felt pointless and artificial. It was my family's poverty and not my gender which had limited me.

All of my parents—biological, adoptive, and courtesy—had *never* accepted biology as my excuse for failure.

Erika's father had taught math at Columbia University before earning billions on Wall Street and moving to Greenwich. I gave Missy his advice when we chose classes.

"Go with the smartest teacher that you can find. You'll learn from them and they'll give you the least trouble since they're sure of their abilities."

"That makes sense. Who said it?" she asked, and I told her.

This sent us on another quest: not for a missing brother but for the best teachers.

We quickly learned the accuracy of another statement of Erika's father. That there are three types of college professors: those who most love teaching, those who most love research, and those who most love themselves.

Those in the last group were to be avoided. They took disagreement personally and hassled students who argued with them. Since career advancement was their major goal, these teachers acquired power by taking on administrative tasks that no one else wanted. Alas, whenever you needed a favor, you were forced into their den.

"I've battled worse," I said, thinking aloud of people in my past who had tried to murder me.

"What?" Missy asked.

"Talking to myself," I mumbled, and she stared at me for a moment.

"I'm OK. It's the stress of being away from home," I said, reassuringly, though feeling that it was probably more than that.

"Take it slow. A girl in Brooks had a seizure yesterday."

"*What*?" I asked, freezing in my tracks.

"A small one. She was talking and began repeating herself. She didn't collapse or froth at the mouth. She caught herself after a few moments and sat down. The others are avoiding her so I invited her to have lunch with us. She said that she hadn't had a seizure in years but the stress of school got to her. So take it easy!"

"OK," I said, simply, and we walked on.

Chapter 18

There was a package on my bed when I returned to my room the next day.

"I picked it up downstairs. It was FedEx'd from Berlin," Missy said, with a look of curiosity.

"It's probably from my dad," I said casually.

"What's he doing in Berlin?"

"He lives there."

"Wait, you have an adoptive father in Greenwich and a biological father in London. How did you get a third father in Berlin?"

An obvious question, I thought.

"Vladimir is my courtesy father and not a real one. He semi-adopted me years ago after I did him a favor and has helped me since. My English dad is a partner in his security business," I said.

"Oh."

The package held presents: an expensive but modestly chic carry-all, thankfully lacking a brand logo which I hate. Being a walking ad isn't my style. The box described it as being a Mansur Gavriel Bucket Bag. I had never heard of the brand but Missy gushed.

"*Wow*," she said, her eyes widening. "What else is in the package?"

A smaller box held a high-tech 18K gold ring with an onyx stone. The instructions said that it would light up and vibrate when my IPhone received a call, a message, or a social-media posting. I would keep it turned off.

The enclosed card read, "Good luck at Barnard. Don't forget to call if you need help..." It was signed, "Your Berlin Parents, Vladimir and Ulrika."

"You're very lucky," Missy said, after reading the note over my shoulder.

You don't know the half of it, I thought.

Our calm was interrupted by a banging on the door. I opened it and Carla, a student from the adjoining suite, burst in. She threw herself on Missy's bed and bawled loudly.

I looked at Missy. She looked at me. We both looked at Carla.

I instantly realized that it would be dumb to ask if something bad had happened. Something obviously had but what?

Horrible events occur but this is Barnard. What could have happened *here*? I wondered. We quickly learned.

"I'm leaving school. I can't stay here *now*!" Carla insisted.

Missy and I looked at each other.

"*OK*," I said slowly to Carla.

No explanation came.

"What happened?" I finally asked.

"What happened? You ask, 'What happened?'"

Missy and I again exchanged glances. This sounded like an all-nighter.

Eventually, Carla told us her story.

Her biology teacher gave a lab demonstration about bacteria. She asked each student to swab their mouth with a q-tip and place the sample of their saliva on a petri dish. It was then sealed, labeled with the student's name, and placed in an incubator.

The next day, each petri dish except one was filled with yellowish colored bacteria. That petri dish held greenish-blue bacteria. The homework was to take a sample of the different specimen home and identify it. This would be done by comparing it with pictures in the textbook.

The only bacteria that matched is one found in semen. Carla had oral sex with her boyfriend a few minutes before class.

I sat beside Carla and placed my hand on her shoulder.

"You're *not* dropping out of school! Loving someone is not a good reason to do that," I said firmly, and that was it.

Carla stopped sobbing. She hugged each of us and left.

"*Wow*," Missy said.

"*Wow*," I repeated.

Chapter 19

Missy and I chose the same classes. This did this mostly to share classwork but also because neither of us had a career in mind. My goal was to marry Randy after we completed college. I would then work at *some* job while he attended graduate school. Missy's goal was to find Odis.

During registration we had learned that two courses were required for all First Year students. One, English, was fine with me so long as I needn't read more of the 19th century English classics that I had loathed in high school. The second class was intended to improve our writing and communication skills and who would argue with these goals.

The catalog descriptions of both classes were so vague that, depending on the teacher, they might be valuable or bullshit. This, though I love to write and have been told that it can be hard to shut me up.

There was a good reason why I chose to attend Barnard apart from its first-rate reputation and being awarded a full scholarship.

My grandmother in London had encouraged me to attend Cambridge University where a friend of my English father taught. But that would have been too far from Randy. Still, my grandmother is wealthy and I might have visited home during school vacations.

Maybe I had made a mistake coming here, I thought. But it was now too late to change school once I had joined Missy on her quest.

Before graduating, students needed classes in nine academic areas. Few of these seemed practical if one hoped to work at anything except waitressing. While Randy attended graduate school, I would be the most literate waitress around.

I shared these thoughts with Missy. She was more optimistic.

"'Find the smartest teacher' is what you said. That still sounds like good advice."

That's what we did. We looked for the sharpest teacher of any subject and hoped for the best.

Thinking that the least muddle-headed people avoided the humanities, we chose the Biology Sequence. It covered cell biology, genetics, evolution, and how germs cause disease and can be used by terrorists.

"You can't get more practical than that," Missy said, and I nodded agreement.

We also signed up for General Chemistry. This taught the basics of gases, solutions, and reactions.

I wanted to add a third class but Missy objected.

"We'll need free time to live," she said.

Once again I recognized that despite Missy's obsession with Odis, her judgment remained good.

We finished registration at a little after 1:00PM. While strolling the campus, deep in conversation with Missy, I absent-mindedly noticed a tall, well-dressed man walking down the steps of the Administration Building. He was engaged in animated conversation with an equally well-dressed woman.

I froze and a boy walking in back brushed against me and apologized.

"What is it?" Missy asked.

"I know that man," I said.

"Oh?" Missy asked, but I ignored her interest.

Ivan was his name. He had saved my life in London. There, he had been the Russian military attaché. He was also a trained killer.

Chapter 20

While Missy gossiped, I considered the man that I had seen. Was it Ivan or had I imagined him? Our encounter in London had been filled with emotion. I even dreamed about him on the plane during my return to America.

Certainly, this man had looked different. He had a different haircut and clothing style. Still, though I wasn't close enough to see his eye color, the shape of his nose and his ears were the same and they can't be changed without surgery. Even his military bearing and walk had been identical to Ivan's.

Yes, it had been Ivan but what was he doing here? I asked myself. Not that he shouldn't be since the Russian government might have posted him to America. He might be visiting Columbia to speak with a noted teacher or to attend a public lecture.

"*Maybe*," I murmured to myself aloud.

"Huh?" Missy asked.

"Talking to myself," I replied.

"You want to watch that," Missy said.

Her tone had been serious and she was right.

We stopped at a bulletin board on our way to the Dining Hall. Notices displayed offers of rides and riders, club activities, and upcoming lectures. Missy pointed to a talk with the intriguing title of "Would You Live as a Boy to Survive?"

"Would you?" she asked.

"I have," I replied.

"You're a continual surprise to me."

"We don't yet know each other that well."

"This story you *must* tell me," Missy insisted.

So I did, after we selected our lunches from amongst the few vegetarian choices.

"It happened when I was in London. My English father was missing-in-action and I tried to learn what he had been like. I read his favorite books and watched his favorite videos. I felt furious that I had never known him.

"I went for a walk to rid myself of this feeling. I was dressed in his raincoat and hat and held his walking stick. A mugger tried to rob me at knife point. He thought I was a boy."

The rage that I had felt that day coursed through me and I couldn't speak. Missy touched my hand.

"It's all right," she said, sympathetically.

I shook my head as if to clear my mind and continued my story.

"I became enraged when I realized what was happening. Did this guy consider me a fool? *He would rob me in broad daylight on a London street?* That was the thought but my anger mostly came from frustration at having never known my biological father.

"I acted frightened and the mugger relaxed. He thought that I would be an easy target. I smashed his nose with the walking stick and then broke his kneecaps. I was *very* angry," I said calmly.

Missy stared at me and it was several moments before she spoke.

"I hope you never get that angry with me. What did you tell the police?"

"Nothing, for there were no police around. The street was deserted and I ran home."

"I would never need a gun with you at my side," Missy said.

"That's not true. A gun is like toilet paper. When you need it, you need it bad."

Again, Missy stared.

That line wasn't mine. It had been told to me by Ulrika, Vladimir's girl-friend and the mother of his infant daughter. She knew about guns, having been an officer in the KSK, the *Kommando Spezialkräfte* or German Special Forces.

After a few moments of thought, Missy looked puzzled.

"But you've said that your English father is alive," she objected.

"Yes, but that was after he returned from the dead," I replied.

Missy looked down and concentrated on eating her melted cheese sandwich. Despite being armed with a pistol, she looked scared.

Chapter 21

Missy would have considered me crazy if I had left my story at that. First saying that my English father was dead and then that he had "returned from the dead." Missy is nervous, keep your explanation simple, I told myself, and that's what I did.

I told her the bare, reassuring facts, leaving out things that would have upset her. As that in addition to being a Mormon, I also practiced the Santeria faith.

"Witchcraft and animal sacrifice–you're into those?" she would undoubtedly ask. This, though the Santeria religion was as much that as was the Mormon religion about sixty-year-old men marrying teenagers.

"My father was sent to sell weapons to a rebel group. The mission failed because of governmental bungling and he was badly hurt. He had a concussion and lost his memory. Being fluent in the native language, he was adopted by a local tribesman as his son, and married.

"Years later, during an attack in which his wife and many in the village were killed, he regained enough memory to notify the British government and was flown back to England.

"Upon arrival, he was in good health except for having huge gaps in his memory. His mother and I helped him recover. Now he's completely OK and is considered a hero.

"That's it and I'm *not* crazy! It was a rough time for many besides us. That was the summer of the London bombing."

"I'm sorry," Missy said.

"It's not your fault."

"No, it's not that, I'm sorry for having doubted you."

"That's OK. We're friends and friends can be crazy with each other," I said, with a smile, and we finished our lunch in silence.

The following days passed quietly. We bought textbooks and met other students. On Sunday, we attended the Mormon Church located several miles south. Getting there involves a comfortable bus ride. Watching the fleeting Broadway scene is always a treat.

The Church service was the usual: singing of hymns followed by prayers offered by members and a partaking of the bread and water communion.

That day there were two speakers and one story had us in tears. A young woman had given birth prematurely. She described her feelings when she was unsure if her son would live. Thankfully he did.

"That's what happened to my friend, Hillary," I whispered to Missy, when the speaker sat down.

"How old was she?"

"Sixteen."

Missy stared but this look was shorter than those she had been giving me. She's getting used to me, I thought.

Being eighteen, we were too old for the Young Women's Group and were shuttled into the Relief Society meeting. Its former name, "Home, Family, and Personal Enrichment," describes its topics. These are so general as to include just about anything.

That day's topic was unusual since having a family is considered a sacred duty in the Mormon Church. But New York City has a huge number of singles. I've read that only Washington, D.C. has a greater percentage.

A girl with short-cut red hair, a red-and-black checkered blouse, a red-and-black jacket, and a black skirt that was much too short for a Mormon service asked a question. Her clothes made it obvious that she wasn't Mormon. Mormons dress conservatively for Church.

The girl asked, "What about single women? Do we even exist in the eyes of the Church?"

Missy and I perked up. This girl sounded like one of us.

The group's leader wasn't flustered. She had a Biblical answer ready since this was probably a common concern in this City. Spending your life attending weddings and baptisms wouldn't improve any single woman's mood. The thought occurred to me that having men attend this group would help relieve the problem. After all, it *was* named the *Relief Society*.

Lacking this resource, the speaker gave a good enough answer. She said that we are all children of God, and that He does not love us less because of our condition no matter what that is. She said that a single woman is no less worthy than those having a husband and children though she may feel that her life has no purpose. She said that many women with children feel overwhelmed by life, have low self-worth, and feel lonely and frustrated.

The speaker said that single women should not build walls to cut themselves off from others who are married. At this point the micro-skirted woman piped up. "And they may know an eligible man too," she said, and everyone laughed. "Yes, very true," the speaker replied, and smiled before continuing.

The speaker concluded by saying that life is more satisfying when we focus on what we have rather than on what we do not have, and that along with our faith we must maintain hope.

It was a satisfying answer and, as usual, I felt better after the meeting. During the refreshment hour that followed, I found myself next to the red-haired woman whose dress had convinced me that she was a stranger to the religion.

"What do you think of the Church?" I asked her.

She glanced at me briefly before replying, then quickly returned her gaze to a man of about twenty. He was conservatively dressed in the dark suit-white shirt-dark tie Mormon missionary custom, and his face held an infectious grin.

"Hmm?" she said, barely registering my question before leaving my side to dart toward him. "I'd certainly convert for *him*."

Chapter 22

Erika's boyfriend, Clarence, is also a bit of a genius like my boyfriend, Randy. Both tend to acquire odd facts. Clarence once said that people are more likely to be caring to members of their own tribe than to strangers. That throughout human history, tribal identity has distinguished "us" from "them."

I thought of this when a church couple invited us to their home for Sunday brunch. But that wasn't how Missy and I wanted to spend the afternoon. It was beautiful weather and we wanted to explore the city. So we thanked them for their kindness and accepted their phone numbers. We promised to visit them, having had no alternative. The wife had been persistent and some people won't take "no" for an answer.

Rather than walk up Broadway toward Barnard, we strolled south toward Times Square. This was the first time that Missy had been to New York City and she glowed with excitement. There is a pedestrian mall with benches at Times Square and we sat for a while viewing the scene. We tried to distinguish the City residents from the tourists and placed obvious families into the latter category.

Several boys tried to pick us up, possibly feeling that we must be easy pickings because of our conservative church-going dress. We smiled but ignored them and they quickly gave up.

We left Times Square and walked east. At Grand Central Station we bought sandwiches at a Subway and ate in the mostly empty waiting room that is reserved for train travelers. But no one asked to see our tickets.

Missy pulled out her IPhone and checked the news. Her daily habit was to Google for Odis. I, and likely she, sensed that this was pointless but the act gave her hope. Just like those who buy lottery tickets, I thought. I chewed as she searched and then read the news.

"What's your English father's name?" she asked, and I told her.

"That's what I thought. He's in the news," she said, handing the phone to me.

People sometimes say that hearing no news is good news but this wasn't bad. To the contrary, the story was a press release about the security firm that my father owns together with Vladimir and a retired CIA official. The company had formed an alliance with the largest personal protection firm in America.

"It's just a business deal," I said, returning the phone to her.

"We can walk to the UN building," I suggested, when we finished eating.

I found myself speaking like a travel guide since I had been to Manhattan many times and Missy hadn't.

"No, I just want to hang-out and watch people," she said, and that was fine with me.

Missy Googled for parks and found one that she liked.

"Greenacre Park on East 51st Street. It has seats, a twenty-five foot waterfall, and a bakery stand."

"You can't beat that," I said.

We left Grand Central Station and walked east toward Second Avenue and then north to 51st Street. The park was as described. An additional attraction is that its waterfall drowns out the City's noise. A custodian discouraged rude behavior, like putting feet on seats.

"We can't sit here without buying anything," Missy said, walking toward the bakery kiosk.

While following her, I decided how much I could afford to spend after having bought lunch. I'll buy a small orange juice, I told myself.

I was about to ask Missy to order this for me when a body wrapped me in a bear hug. I was unable to move as a mouth whispered in my ear, "How delightful."

I'm being molested. Should I scream? I asked myself.

Chapter 23

Among the best advice that I learned from my self-defense lessons is that if a man comes at you, there is one sure way to take him out. It works every time if he doesn't know how to look for it. You hit him with the heel of your palm, bringing it hard up into his nose. If powerful enough, your blow will drive splinters from his nasal cartilage into his brain and kill him instantly.

The grip holding me was so powerful that struggling against it would have been useless. So I relaxed my body and the man released me. Then I clenched my hand and whirled, hoping to break his nose by smashing my palm into it. The man was quicker. He caught my hand and smiled.

"Did I not say that Margaret is dangerous? She is truly Vladimir's daughter," the man said, smiling to his companion.

"Ivan," I screeched.

I threw my arms around his neck as my eyes watered from relief and the joy of seeing him. A year earlier, he had saved my life in London.

It *was* Ivan that I had seen on campus, I told myself, and he had been with the same woman though the boy who now accompanied them was a stranger. He was also gorgeous: tall and black haired, with the chiseled features of a Greek God. He is triple your image of Ansel Elgort.

"What are you doing here?" I asked Ivan.

"Margaret, this is my wife, Dina, and my son, Artur. He just began study at Columbia," Ivan said.

I introduced Missy and all smiled and shook hands. Artur couldn't take his eyes off Missy. Her face and soft Southern drawl has that effect on men. Without further thought, they want to take her home forever.

People were staring. My martial movement had created a scene that even blasé New Yorkers couldn't ignore.

"We have lunch reservations. Come with us," Dina said.

"There are vegetable dishes," Ivan added, when I hesitated.

Vegetarians, like me and Missy, feel uncomfortable when they're trapped in a dining situation at which there is little for them to eat.

I looked toward Missy. She nodded slightly.

"We would love to," I said.

Ivan phoned the restaurant and said that there would be two more guests for lunch. The Russian Samovar is directly across town from the park, on 52nd Street between Broadway and 8th Avenue. Ivan and Dina led the way, as parents tend to do, while Artur and Missy and I followed.

Though accented and occasionally stilted, Artur's English was excellent. I was pleased that he paid most of his attention to Missy. I already had a boyfriend and she deserved happiness. But I feared that she would break his heart.

The restaurant had an old world feel. As soon as we entered, the manager greeted Ivan with a hug and a Russian greeting that I couldn't understand. I've learned a little Russian from Erika's Russian bodyguards but not much. These are common Russian greetings and other statements that they had playfully taught me like "I love you" ("Ya tibya a publyu") and "I really like it" ("Mne eta ochin' nr avitsa!"). You get the idea.

The restaurant's tables were close together and the room was noisy with Russian songs. This was heightened by the loud talk from customers celebrating at a large table nearby.

Ivan sat beside his wife, Artur and Missy sat opposite them, and I looked the odd one out though I didn't mind.

Despite the waiting crowd, we had been seated instantly and the waiter couldn't do enough for us. Ivan ordered cranberry vodka for himself and Dina, and looked toward us expectantly.

"We're Mormon and don't drink," I said.

Upon hearing our decision, Artur also refused. He suggested, "Juice?" and his parents smiled with understanding. Artur's mind was already occupied with Missy. Food was the last thing on his mind as our lunch began.

Chapter 24

Missy was mostly quiet throughout the lunch. She smiled and answered questions but the facts that she shared weren't personal. She described her impression of Manhattan and compared it with her former life down South. But she said nothing of her family or Odis' disappearance.

Missy re-adopted the role of cheerleader and Homecoming Queen that she had been: beautiful and impersonally friendly. A boy might lust but not imagine dating her for she would be felt to be far above him.

But though Missy had been Homecoming Queen, Artur's looks could easily have made him Homecoming King. I wondered how much studying he would manage after the Barnard girls discovered him. They would offer to do his school work and laundry and anything else. Girls from the wealthier families might propose a lifetime of leisure.

Yet, I sensed that Artur was no playboy. He said that he was taking a dual major in biology and math. He loved both subjects but was unsure what he would do. His parents' eyes shone with pride as he spoke. Their love for him was evident.

I said that I wasn't sure what I would do after college except to get married.

"Artur doesn't have a girlfriend," Ivan said, impishly, and I smiled and said that I was already chosen.

It was clear that Artur was already hooked on Missy. Fearing that his obvious question was coming—and that it would upset her—I rambled on about my life. Missy had told me that she would never love until finding Odis.

"I've known my boyfriend, Randy, since we were kids and we've dated since we were thirteen. He's studying pre-med at Yale. We Skype nearly every day."

"Artur wants to be a doctor too," Dina said, with interest.

"No, he'll never be a doctor," I said with a small laugh.

"Then why is he taking pre-med?" Artur asked, this most logical question.

"*That's* a story. Randy's father is a doctor. He's paying Randy's college expenses for him to become a doctor though Randy faints at the sight of blood. His father hoped that he would get over this by witnessing his sister's birth. I caught Randy before he hit the floor. He wound up in the bed next to his mother and became a hospital-wide joke.

"Randy is taking pre-med classes to please his father but also as much math and computer science as he can fit into his schedule. He wants to get a Ph.D. after graduating. We'll hide out in Utah where I have family and his father can't get at him."

When I finished speaking, everyone at the table except Missy smiled and I smiled too.

I turned toward Artur.

"It's a dopey situation. You should meet him. I think you and Randy could become friends," I added.

"I'd like to," Artur replied, as our food arrived.

Missy and I had chosen the same appetizer of Garden Salad with olive oil. As a main dish, I had the Smoked Salmon (salmon, chopped eggs, onion, dill, and Russian mustard) and she had the Red Caviar Napoleon (salmon roe, smoked salmon, crepes, and goat cheese).

For dessert we had Pastila, small squares of pressed fruit paste, and Tula gingerbread, a cookie made with honey and having the Coat of Arms of Russia. We drank bottled water.

Our food's authenticity explained why few of the diners appeared to be American.

Chapter 25

"Do you have plans for the afternoon?" Dina asked, as we left the restaurant.

I looked toward Missy but couldn't read her expression.

"No," I replied.

"*Wonderful!* We can walk a bit and you can see our apartment."

"You have an apartment in Manhattan?" I asked, with surprise, knowing that the cost of City real estate had gone through the roof.

Ivan is a Russian military attaché. He was probably doing more than simply keeping track of American weaponry but the last that I heard he had been stationed in London.

"It's leased by Vladimir's company but he's generous and loans it out. He suggested that Artur live there while attending Columbia but Artur wants the campus experience. The apartment is just across town, on East 58th Street," Dina explained. "There's a lovely park along the way that you must see. It has a waterfall like at the other park," she added.

This park is on Sixth Avenue between 48th and 49th Streets. Now it's one thing to sit beside rushing water and another thing to walk through it. This waterfall is part of the McGraw-Hill building and within a small plaza connecting the two streets. To get from one street to the other, you enter a Plexiglas tunnel with water plunging around you.

Walking through it went slowly because people tended to cluster and take photos. A girl of about our age, Helga, was part of a German family of five. She asked Artur to take their picture. When he returned her smartphone, Helga hugged him, thanked him effusively, and took his picture. She offered to take a picture of our group but Ivan smiled and said that *he* would take a photo of all of us. The thought passed through my mind that Ivan didn't want his picture taken.

Helga asked Artur for his E-mail address to send the photo that she had taken of him. I wondered what other photos she might send. Yes, Artur is *that* good looking!

I looked at Missy to see if she was jealous but her expression was unreadable. She protects herself by not showing what she feels. Her damned-up emotions are too strong, I thought.

The apartment was in a building that is pretentiously named Le Triomphe. There, residents could enjoy The Club which contained a lounge, a dining/conference room, a children's playroom, a three-thousand foot fitness facility with state-of-the-art aerobics and strength training machines, and an indoor pool with sun decks.

In short, if you didn't need to shop for food and other things and had friends living in the building you could remain indoors and be happy.

Once past the granite-filled lobby with its muted lighting and sofas, we rode an artfully decorated elevator to their 27th floor apartment.

It contained all that any reasonable person could demand in an apartment. The rooms and balconies were large for Manhattan and the views were spectacular.

The apartment was a decorator furnished, two-bedroom, two-bathroom affair. Dina took Missy and I through it while Artur spoke with his father in the living room.

Having been leased already furnished, the apartment was comfortable but impersonal. The living room floors were hardwood. An abstract patterned rug covered the seating area which contained an orange leather sofa, a coffee table, and two club chairs. Other chairs were close by the large windows. A beige/white abstract painting hung above the sofa.

A flat-screen TV sat atop a table and in another corner was a marble-topped dining room table surrounded by six chairs.

The kitchen was white and contained the usual microwave, oven, refrigerator, and dishwasher.

All of the bedroom furniture including the rugs were in shades of white, brown, and beige, and both bedrooms held a king-size bed. The walls were white as were all of the bathroom fixtures. Its bright lighting highlights every blemish, I thought.

There was bottled water and juice and cheese and crackers on the coffee table in the living room when we returned.

As we munched and relaxed, Dina said, "The neutral furniture causes the apartment to look empty, as if no one lived here."

Now Missy spoke for the first time since we had left the restaurant. Her brief comment was so private that it shocked us into silence.

"Like my heart," she said softly.

Chapter 26

I didn't know what to say. Neither did any of the others. For a girl to state that her heart is empty usually means that she doesn't have a beloved. But I knew what Missy was really saying for she had told me earlier: that she would be unable to love until finding Odis, who she remained convinced was alive.

Erika, my go-to-girl about feelings based on her years of therapy, once told me that it's normal for a person to feel depressed after losing someone they loved. When viewed this way, Missy's feeling was normal. Odis had been her oldest brother and had parented her for half of her life. Missy felt as I would if I had lost a parent. But it was worse for her since I would have Randy to fill my heart.

When a person says something puzzling, people either ignore the remark or ask for an explanation. Artur and his parents did the former, sensing that Missy wouldn't welcome questions.

I said that we had to leave to do homework, which is always a believable excuse. Artur remained with his parents. We invited him to visit us and he said that he would. I felt sorry for him for his heart would be broken.

"Do you want to take the subway or bus?" I asked Missy, as we left the apartment building.

"The subway. We can walk across town. I need to think," she replied.

Margaret of Greenwich

We walked across 57th Street to the West Side and then to the 7th Avenue subway station at 59th Street. We would take the train to the 116th Street stop, a few blocks from campus.

Manhattan seems strange after growing up in a small town. At first you walk with your head gazing upwards toward the tops of the buildings you pass. But you soon stop this since it is dangerous when crossing a street.

Another thing that you quickly learn is not to dawdle while walking. New Yorkers move fast and one must keep up with the pedestrian flow or be trampled. I had been to the City many times and gotten used to this custom but Missy was a newcomer and absent-minded too. After several near collisions, I seized her arm and increased our pace.

"How soon before Randy calls?" Missy asked, after a few minutes of silence.

"As soon as he finds something but I'll call him when we get back," I replied.

At the subway station entrance, Missy changed her mind.

"I need more time to think. Let's walk home," she said.

I readily agreed though Brooks Hall was three miles away. I love to walk and had put on two pounds since arriving on campus. I like eating and being on a meal-plan where one need not worry about the cost of food...Well, you can imagine.

"OK, but tell me if you get tired. We can take the bus the rest of the way," I said.

We walked silently for another three or four blocks before Missy spoke.

"I haven't told you something," she said, hesitantly.

"Hmm..." I replied, briefly.

Her tone hadn't invited questions.

"Yes," Missy said.

"Hmm..." I repeated.

"Yes," Missy repeated.

It took another two blocks before Missy told me what was on her mind.

"I'm pregnant," she said, in a barely audible voice.

Chapter 27

We were waiting to cross the street, choking on the noxious fumes from a passing truck when Missy dropped her bombshell,

I stopped dead in my tracks as the truck moved on but Missy continued walking. When I caught up with her, thinking that I must have misheard, I could only screech "*What*?"

"I'm about seven weeks along, have an April baby. Maybe that's what I should name her," she said, with a tone that bordered on hysteria.

"We need a drink," was all that I could stammer.

It wasn't what I ever say but Mormons have bad days too. There was a Starbucks on the corner. We sat there, side by side.

"Do your parents know?" I asked.

As reply, I received a look indicating that mine had been a dumb question. Publicizing one's pregnancy requires planning. Judging by Missy's emotional state, her pregnancy had shocked her and it wasn't a happy surprise either.

I sipped my juice as Missy stared out the window. She remained silent, thinking.

"Have you told the baby's father?" I asked.

"That's not possible," Missy replied.

I tried to control myself so my face wouldn't reveal the shock that I felt. People make decisions about others. These are based on their appearance and what is known about them. Erika once explained this as reflecting the mind's tendency to speed up its decision making. Thus, people are placed in pre-formed categories with reactions being made as they were to similar people in the past.

I had automatically placed Missy into a category. She had been a cheer-leader and was the daughter of a Mormon bishop with all that demanded.

While I hadn't considered her sex life, I had believed that she was a virgin like me, and most of my best friends too. Hillary is the exception. She had discovered sex at twelve and was pregnant by fifteen.

I suddenly felt nervous. If my conclusions about Missy were so wrong, could I ever trust them again? Then I calmed down. I *did* know Missy but just not everything about her. And how was I expected to since I had known her so briefly?

Moreover, how early one had sex tells you nothing about their nature. Hillary is now a dedicated mother, which one wouldn't have expected considering how self-centered she had been.

Following that reasoning, I stopped being critical. Who the baby's father is wasn't important. What was, was how I could help her and that's what I said.

"I'm your friend and will support you whatever you decide," I promised.

Margaret of Greenwich

Missy began crying softly, and my eyes watered too.

Chapter 28

We walked more slowly after leaving Starbucks. Missy had decisions to make and these take time. Should she inform the baby's father? Should she have the child and, if so, keep it or place it for adoption? Should she tell her parents now and what would their likely reaction be?

This answer was easiest since her father was a Mormon bishop. We knew the Church's official policies on sex and abortion but also, as with other religions, that these were frequently ignored by its members. The smiling, child-laden families that we passed didn't make Missy's decision easier.

"What would you do?" she asked me.

I scanned passersby: tourists unsuccessfully trying to look like New Yorkers and residents trying to be more of themselves. Only after a half-block of walking did I feel comfortable answering her imposing question.

"I'd have the baby. Not because I consider abortion wrong since it's every woman's right to decide and definitely not the business of politicians. But once the fertilized egg began growing, I'd feel it was part of me. Ridding myself of it would be removing part of my body."

Now it was Missy's term to abruptly halt and face me.

"That's *exactly* what I feel. So it's decided," she said, with a monumental lack of clarity.

"*OK*. Exactly what is it that you plan to do?" I asked.

There was a long pause before Missy answered. I could almost see her brain working.

"I'm not sure. When you spoke I agreed with you so completely that I decided to keep the baby. But when this feeling passes, I'll probably think of all the difficulties this will cause. I'm financially dependent on my parents. They won't be sympathetic, and will insist on knowing the baby's father."

"Who is he?" I asked, after nodding agreement with her conclusions.

"My high school guidance counselor. We're been lovers since I was fifteen," Missy answered.

Thankfully, we hadn't been in the street at risk of being run over when Missy dropped this surprise. Again, I stopped in my tracks. This is becoming a habit. It would be safer holding this conversation in our room, I told myself.

"*Since you were fifteen? For three years?*" I asked, in astonishment and so loudly that bystanders stared.

I'd known of girls who had affairs with their teachers but these had been brief flings. *Three years?*

We were still a mile from campus and I needed to rest. I was psychologically drained. One can take only so much. I steered Missy toward a coffee shop. There is one on nearly every other block in Manhattan.

Once there, I ordered a toasted cinnamon-raisin bagel and juice while Missy ordered a plain toasted bagel and milk. Her pregnancy is already affecting her behavior, I thought. I waited until the food arrived before speaking.

"Tell me about it," I said, in the softest tone that I could muster.

"OK, but don't judge me. You can't judge anyone until you've walked in their shoes."

I nodded agreement though having doubts. One can't experience everything and God gave us a mind to think logically and consider consequences. Still, when considering the events of my life, I should be about the last person to judge anyone.

"Missy, you don't know what I've done," I said firmly, placing my hand over her's. "*Nothing* that you can say will change our friendship."

Chapter 29

My bagel and juice lay uneaten while Missy spoke. I let her speak without interruption. Doing otherwise would have been impossible. Once she began speaking it was like a dam had burst.

I felt that Missy had hungered to tell her story but had no one to tell it to. Her father was a Mormon bishop, her mother was a bishop's wife, and one doesn't tell a brother of such things.

"I would have told Odis but he was gone and I was alone," Missy explained.

"It began innocently. My grades had dropped and the guidance counselor was doing research on students who weren't doing as well as they should be according to their intelligence. My parents had their kids tested when we were young. My IQ is 149, the highest of all," she said, with a touch of pride.

"Thirty of us were involved in the research, half boys and half girls. We took psychological tests and spoke with him alone. He asked about our life and whether anything was bothering us. Two of my friends were in this project and they told me that they had denied being unhappy. I might have been the only one to tell the truth. I couldn't hold back. I had felt alone for so long.

"I told him–Jerry–about Odis' disappearance and the birthday charm that I still received and how I was the only person convinced that he was alive. Jerry was the only person to take what I said seriously. Everyone else thought that I was…well…crazy.

"Jerry said that he believed me and we began meeting every week. I talked about everything though I sometimes wondered how he had the patience to listen. I mean, how exciting is high school drama to any grownup?

"He shared things too, and he took my opinions seriously. He and his wife had been childhood sweethearts. He wanted children but she didn't so they were a bad match from the start. It took time for them to realize how bad their relationship was but once they did it was over. They still slept together but hadn't had sex in five years though she had sex with others."

At this revelation, I couldn't contain myself.

"He told you about his sex life?" I asked, with a hint of incredulity.

"Not right away, and we didn't have sex until I was fifteen. Before that we just talked," Missy said, with a shrug.

Missy paused, drank some milk, and began ripping the inside of the bagel from its crust, discarding the white and eating the crust.

"I only like the crust," she explained.

For some reason this habit disgusts me though I had seen other girls do it. But I said nothing.

After eating half the bagel and drinking more milk, Missy continued her story.

"Judging by what I did, you may think me stupid but I'm not. I knew our relationship was crazy but I needed someone and there was no one except him. Is it wrong to want love?"

No, it isn't wrong to love and it wasn't your fault that you had sex with him. He was an adult and you were a child and he groomed you for the relationship, I thought.

I didn't say this, which she must already have concluded, but simply nodded. Instead, I asked, "Do you still love him?"

Missy put down the bagel and swallowed hard before answering. Her beautiful face contorted into something ugly and that I had never seen before. I knew that she didn't want to tell what she was about to say but that she had to. She was in a confessing mood and I had become her confessor.

"I'll *always* love Jerry but he is dead and I killed him," she said.

Chapter 30

Sentences have slightly different meanings depending on how each word is emphasized. Compare "*I* love you" with "I love *you*." But though trying hard, I couldn't think of a different way to interpret Missy's statement, "I killed him."

I looked around the coffee shop to give myself time to think though it was the kind of place where you avoid looking at people. In a small town your interest would receive a smile but not in large cities. I've heard of people being shot for less. An obvious pimp did smile but I looked away quickly,

I turned toward Missy.

"You killed him?" I asked.

"He's dead, isn't he?"

"OK, but did you *murder* him?" I repeated.

"Well, not exactly," Missy replied.

Getting information from her was starting to feel like getting facts from a five-year-old.

"Tell me about it," I said, in a firm no-nonsense tone, and she did.

"His house was a mile from ours so getting together was easy, after school or on weekends. We even had a few sleepovers though that was risky—you could never be sure who might see me coming or leaving. But we were careful. I avoided him in school and never mentioned his name. If a friend did, I acted as if I didn't know him.

"It was me who pushed us having sex though he didn't exactly object. My body wanted it. It was as simple as that."

Not quite so simple, I thought, but didn't say.

"By then, his wife had left him and we became like an ordinary married couple if you consider it normal that we couldn't be seen together. He talked about his friends and I talked about my friends and we talked about our future. We planned to marry after I finished college or maybe when I was midway through it. There's no rule against being married and attending Barnard, is there?"

"I have no idea," I replied.

I was trying to keep my tone neutral at the craziness she was describing. I wanted to keep her talking.

"He didn't like working at the school. He hated the dumb rules and wanted to start his own business. He was a state trooper before becoming a guidance counselor. He left the police after he had to beat up a man he was arresting. He *couldn't stand* hurting people. He became a counselor to help kids who were hurting."

I shook my head at Missy's naiveté. Her story was getting even stranger.

"Jerry said that he wanted to open a private investigative agency in Atlanta or another big city. He promised to help me find Odis!"

Missy's eyes watered. You poor sap, I couldn't help thinking.

"Jerry really loved me and I loved him too despite the difference in our ages. Today, that doesn't matter so much. Many women marry older men and he wasn't yet forty. He even wrote me poetry."

Missy pulled her smartphone from her backpack. She handed me headphones so I could listen to his lines that she had recorded:

"Let us, though late, wed at last,

And loving lie in one devoted bed.

No sound calls back the year that once is past.

Then, sweetest Missy, let's no longer stay,

True love, we know, causes delay.

Away with doubts, all scruples hence remove!

No man, and one time, can be wise, and love."

"Isn't it beautiful?" Missy asked, and I nodded.

"He read it to me before we first had sex. Now you understand the kind of man he was," Missy said.

I sure did! The Greenwich High School English teachers *love* the classical English authors, a sentiment that few of their students share. I immediately recognized

Jerry's poem as having been plagiarized, with needed changes, from "To Sylvia, To Wed" by Robert Herrick.

Herrick was a famous 17th English poet who wrote over twenty-five-hundred poems with basically the same message: the world and love are beautiful and we must make the most of it. Jerry and he might have been good friends.

Chapter 31

At this point I felt like say, "Missy, can we cut to the chase: Did you kill Jerry or not?" But I didn't. I still followed my dad's advice to let a person tell their story in their own way. I had tried his patience too. So I sat back and noshed on my bagel, waiting for the facts to dribble out.

"Late one Monday night, after we had a *fabulous* weekend, I went to his house to surprise him. I had baked a strawberry frosted chocolate cake for the family though it was really for him since it was his favorite. I made sure to save a quarter of it for him. I took it to my room on a paper plate covered with two sheets of waxed paper and placed it in my book bag."

These unnecessary details were getting to me but I remained silent. I just nodded and maintained my idiot smile.

"I told my mother that I had to go to a girlfriend's house because I forgot to get the homework. I said I would get up early to do it. Then I left and went to Jerry's house. I expected that most of his lights would be out since he went to bed early. I planned to leave the cake on the kitchen table with a note."

Now, I didn't nod but simply said, "Uh, huh." I had an idea what happened next.

"I had a key and entered the house quietly, not wanting to wake him. I heard sounds upstairs and went to say 'hello' since he seemed to be up. The bedroom door was open and I peeked. He wasn't helping the naked girl with her homework!

"I tiptoed out, and the next day I went to see him in school. I returned the key and told him what I had seen. I said that I would tell my father and the police though I wouldn't have since if I did I'd be wrecking my life too. But I was so angry! I had needed someone and now had no one. I was alone again."

"It's not your fault," I said, with real sympathy. "You were a child and he was an adult. He groomed you for what he wanted. But how did he die?"

"No one knows, or is even sure that he's dead. They found his empty boat drifting along the river. Pinned inside was a note saying that he'd been depressed for a long time. The current is swift and the police concluded that his body drifted downstream or an alligator did away with it. They don't expect to find it.

"Over two hundred people came to his memorial service. I didn't go, and left for Barnard."

"Why do you blame yourself for his death or possible death?" I asked.

"Because he'd still be alive if I hadn't threatened to tell."

"And still preying on teenagers," I said.

"I guess..." Missy replied, in a sad, regretful tone.

The little dope still loves him, I thought.

Chapter 32

"I'm exhausted. Let's take a bus back," Missy said, and I nodded agreement. It had been a killing afternoon and Missy seemed tired beyond any expression of emotion.

We had just stood to leave when the pimp who had been staring at us approached.

"Can I help, ladies? You don't look local," he said.

The man had a gold-crowned grin and, though the day was sunny, he carried the kind of fancy umbrella that I hadn't seen since leaving London. Its handle was wood and the fabric was tweed check. The umbrella seemed part of his "uniform," it having nothing to do with the weather.

"Thanks, but we're students and have to get back," I said, remaining courteous.

"Students, *huh*! School is expensive. How would you like to earn some *real* money?" he asked, with a sly undertone.

Missy's face tightened. Considering how angry she was about Jerry and that she carried a pistol, I feared her exploding in more ways than one. I knew that the pimp's comment was nothing person, for him we were just business, but we felt enraged. Missy had already been pimped, so to speak.

I reacted before she could.

"No, thanks, we have to leave," I said.

I grabbed Missy's arm and hurried us outside.

She briefly resisted but then followed me woodenly, as a child does their mother. She seemed to have become like the character in a play of her creation that nobody understood. Trying to survive from one moment to the next, seeing things but not recognizing them.

While waiting for the bus, we scanned pedestrian's faces with exaggerated suspicion. Finally, Missy relaxed.

"Maybe we should have listened to him. We *do* need money," Missy said, with a grin.

"He might have been a slaver and we'd wind up who knows where," I retorted, adopting her mood before becoming serious.

"You have decisions to make and not much time to make them," I said softly.

Missy didn't reply for the bus had just arrived. We took a two-seater at the back.

I could have said many things but felt she already knew them. She was smart and had lived a complex life. So I sat silently as the bus poked its way through the traffic.

Missy spoke as the bus approached our stop.

"I can't stand anyone now. Can you grab some food and bring it to the room?"

"Sure," I replied.

In the cafeteria, I made two pita sandwiches of grilled salmon and vegetables, added apples and bananas and milk cartons, and brought these to our room. Missy lay on the bed with her arm across her eyes. I placed the food on the desk.

Another bit of advice from my father was that when he wants to relax an upset client, he tells them a story from his legal experiences. This reassures them by showing that others have survived weighty difficulties. Missy was distraught. I decided to tell her a story.

Chapter 33

I've had a difficult life and could have told Missy of many painful events. That which I chose occurred most recently, during my summer in London.

"I know what you must be feeling," I began.

"How can you?" Missy asked, suspiciously.

"Because there have been times in my life that I've felt desperate too."

Missy removed her arm from her eyes and looked at me.

Without intending to, I began crying and it wasn't an act.

"What?" Missy asked.

"I'm sorry, it's just that I've been through so much," I replied.

After wiping my eyes, I told her.

"I've always felt rootless, as if I didn't quite belong in this world. This isn't an unusual feeling for adoptees even if their adoptive parents were totally great as mine were. In fact it was because they were so good, that they seemed to treat me better than my sisters, which caused me to wonder about my origin. And that in my family only I have blue eyes and red hair."

Missy sat up in bed.

"I didn't learn my origin all at once. It dribbled out little-by-little. First, that the woman who I had always called Aunt Lena was my biological mother. Then, that my biological father had been a British spy who was believed to have been killed.

"My parents never married and Lena became pregnant before his death. For her safety, she was advised by the British government to return to America and she did. After my birth, she felt too depressed to raise me. She allowed her sister to adopt me with everyone agreeing to keep my adoption secret.

Missy's eyes had widened as I spoke. This really *is* some story, I told myself.

"My English grandmother began searching for me sixteen months ago. Why she waited so long and Lena didn't tell her of my birth is another story. Grandma found me in Greenwich, we spoke, and she invited me to spend the summer with her in London. There, a miracle happened, and I almost died."

Mormons believe in miracles. The Miracle of the Gulls is a staple of our religion. It describes how, in 1848, seagulls saved the first harvest of the Mormon pioneers by eating thousands of insects that were devouring their crops.

While this story is Mormon folklore, I don't see my story entering it since it involves the Santeria religion upon which many don't look kindly. I left this part out of my story. Missy was fragile and confused enough. Had I told her the whole truth, she would not have trusted me.

"My father had stayed with his mother whenever he was in London. After he was declared dead, she kept his room almost as a shrine. In it I found his old clothes and favorite books and videos. I even discovered his last, unfinished letter to Lena.

"While in his room, I prayed for his spirit as it wandered amongst the dead and had a powerful experience during which my period came early. A week later we learned that he was alive and the government flew him home. He had been amnesic for sixteen years but is now totally OK and a national hero. I finally have my real parents."

We were both crying when I finished speaking. It had been that kind of a day.

Chapter 34

We sat silently for a while before eating. Thankfully, Missy did recover her appetite. Helping a healthy pregnant friend is one thing but aiding a pregnant friend who refuses to care for herself is a whole other ballgame. My friend, Hillary, though being as flaky as they come, had behaved sensibly during her pregnancy. She is now a wonderful mother, as I hoped that Missy would be if she decided to keep her baby.

I didn't ask her this biggest question since I wouldn't have trusted her answer. She was feeling too shaky and was too easily swayed. She might tell me the answer that she felt I wanted to hear, or its opposite as angry kids and grownups often do.

Wait and be her friend and see what comes, both of my fathers seemed to advise me. So that's what I did.

We went to sleep early. When I awoke it was to the sight of Missy, standing in bra and thong, staring at herself sideways in the mirror that hung from the closet door. She was obviously checking to see if she "showed." That didn't surprise me but her thong underwear did. Either her mother is more easy-going than mine or she doesn't know about it, I thought.

"Do I?" Missy asked, noting that I was watching her.

"No. You won't for a while and you can conceal it then. My friend did this successfully for months. I spoke with her nearly every day and never suspected."

"Hmm..." Missy said, thinking as she put on a robe, apparently not yet having decided what to do.

It was Monday and the first day of the fall term. We had dressed in our usual: me, in shirt, jeans, and sneakers; she, in a black top, jeans, low heel shoes, and a multi-patterned, multi-colored sweater that complemented her hair and eye color but was too "busy" for mine.

I said nothing about Missy's fashion. She, after a deliberately brief stare, said nothing about mine though her look's meaning was evident: You're going to class dressed like *that*?

I'd seen that look before. Greenwich is the richest town in America and my family is one of their poorest. It hadn't always been like that but, like they say, shit happens. To which I add, and the smell lingers for a long time though I'd gotten few nasty remarks. This might have been because my best friend is Erika. She's the daughter of the local billionaire and a power in her own right.

I ignored Missy's unspoken words: my cheap clothes were far less of a burden than what she carried.

The hunger that I had felt lessened considerably by the time we reached the entrance to the Dining Hall in the Hewitt basement. We had been walking behind two girls whose major interest in food seemed its safety.

"Bacterial growth is constant and reproduces exponentially. If food is kept too warm, dangerous bacteria grow and grow!" asserted one girl.

"And who guarantees that the workers wash their hands. Many can barely speak English. Have you seen the nails of these women, and forget the men!

"There were flies on the counter the other day and you know what attracts them," said the other girl, neither of whom I knew.

"Shit!" came the simultaneous, laughing statement of both.

We slowed our gait until their voices died off in the distance.

Chapter 35

I noted Missy's choice of food for breakfast– that she was still eating healthfully–and then forgot the matter. It was her baby and she would have to make her own choices. A friend, no matter how good, can do only so much.

Moreover, I had my own worries, the biggest of which was getting good grades. My full scholarship, which was worth a quarter million dollars for all four years, was granted year-to-year and could be revoked for having poor grades, breaking college rules, or whatever.

As a paying student, Missy had fewer worries—so long as no one learned of her gun, of course. Her pregnancy would be considered a lesser sin and how this would be handled by the college was anyone's guess. She might become a Biology Class heroine.

But worrying unnecessarily had never been my style. To again quote my lawyer-father: Don't worry until you have something to worry about! He wasn't present to advise me but after living with him all of my life I was pretty sure what his advice would be in most situations.

Our 9AM class that day was the required First Year English. The course's description stated that we would analyze "the thematic structure of literary works through close reading and translating critical reading into elegant and persuasive expository writing" which included "conducting sources and incorporating scholarship into original analytical arguments" while taking care to "avoid plagiarism and other academic violations of Barnard's Honor Code."

From these efforts we would "develop a sense of literary history," "gain confidence in speaking and writing skills," and "appreciate the value of incisive writing." This would, presumably, make us superior women. Having a healthy pregnancy wasn't mentioned.

There were twenty-four students in the class. Their stylish clothes and carefully applied makeup were little different from that at Greenwich High School. And, just like there, several students were engaged with their tablets and phones. But unlike in high school this teacher didn't mind. She had her laptop open and occasionally glanced toward it. It's the digital age and so long as you do your assignments the rest is up to you, seemed her attitude. Freedom at last though I had long behaved freely.

The teacher, Dr. Chu, looked to be in her late twenties and was nervous. I had heard that she was new so this might be her first class at Barnard. Still, college isn't high school where kids can give teachers a hard time. Dr. Chu's concern about gaining tenure, which depended on producing scholarly publications and not teaching, was years away.

"I'd like to begin by learning the books that you enjoyed and which influence your life. Ideas can be powerful weapons."

Dr. Chu waited silently. Hands slowly raised. The replies shocked me though she seemed unaffected. The girls spoke of popular teenage titles: *The Hunger Games*, *The Fault In Our Stars*, and the like. *This*, at elite Barnard! I thought.

Feeling ashamed for them and worse for Dr. Chu, I raised my hand to put in my two cents.

"Yes?" Dr. Chu asked, hopefully.

"A biography of Dietrich Bonhoeffer," I said, and Dr. Chu smiled broadly.

Then, without conscious thought, my eyes filled with tears and I looked down. Other students stared as emotion swept through me. Though managing to keep my cool, I was unable to hide my feelings. Dr. Chu spoke first.

"Do the rest of you know who Dietrich Bonhoeffer was?" she asked.

Only a few hands went up and Dr. Chu explained.

"He was an eminent Protestant theologian who was executed for opposing Hitler. He lectured at Columbia's Union Theological Seminary. They begged him to remain in America but he insisted on returning to Germany, saying that he couldn't live in his defeated nation unless he had done his part to battle Nazism. He was a great man."

Dr. Chu turned toward me.

"Why were so deeply affected by his life?" she asked, softly.

I remained puzzled and was speechless for several moments until it hit me.

"Because he reminds me of my father," I said, and began crying.

Chapter 36

I've done the unthinkable by crying in class. Girls are expected to be strong. Men don't cry when they're upset and women shouldn't either. That's the beginning and end of my reputation here, I told myself.

But that's not what happened. Missy put her arm around me as another student's hand touched my shoulder.

"Do you want to tell us about it?" Dr. Chu asked, as all eyes in the classroom riveted on me.

For whatever reason, I did. Not everything that had happened in London but just a little so they knew me. A line went through my mind from something that I read: Secrets corrode the soul. I looked up.

"I'm adopted. I first met my biological father last summer in London. Everyone had believed him to be dead but he had amnesia for sixteen years. He had been a British spy and when he recovered his memory and the government learned of his existence, he was flown home and is now a national hero."

My tears flowed again but at that moment I didn't feel ashamed.

Dr. Chu immediately began speaking, to give me time to compose myself.

"Do any of you now doubt the importance of books?" she asked, and no hands were raised.

"Are you alright?" Missy whispered to me.

"Yes, these feelings hit me times. I've been through too much," I whispered back, wiping my eyes and taking a deep breath.

I looked up, smiled, and appeared to listen attentively to Dr. Chu for the remainder of the class. But I couldn't concentrate for I sensed that something was wrong. I didn't know exactly what except that it had to do with Missy.

"Trust your reptilian instincts. They've protected humankind since its beginnings and will get you through," Vladimir had told me. I did, and they had saved my life in the past.

The class ended and Dr. Chu approached me at the door.

"Thank you for being so revealing. You've moved the class forward," Dr. Chu said.

I made a meek smile.

"Some of my experiences I'd much rather have read about," I said.

Chapter 37

Have you ever felt that something bad is about to happen but you have no idea what? A vague unease that won't go away no matter how much you try to push it from your mind. A feeling that you are beginning to move through a nightmare. That's what I felt toward the end of the English class, as if doom were approaching.

I can still remember a student screaming toward another as we left the building. Trivialities tend to affix themselves onto one's mind at times of high tension.

We had a two hour break before our next class. Missy and I returned to our room. I was silent all the way there.

"What's wrong? Is it because of what you said in class?" Missy asked.

"No. I felt uncomfortable for a while but am OK. What I said sounded personal but wasn't: my dad's story was big news last summer. He's even gotten offers to make a movie based on his life."

"Well, what is it then?" Missy persisted.

"I feel something is wrong but don't know what. I'll call around," I said.

I began by phoning my parents. They were glad to hear from me but surprised that I had called so soon after my call on the previous day. That call lasted the longest since I couldn't speak with them without also speaking with each of my three sisters.

My calls to Hillary and Erika followed. I talked about Barnard, Hillary talked of her daughter, and Erika talked of her boyfriend. Everything was going fine with them too.

It's probably just my edginess about school, I told myself, as I dialed Randy's number. My call went to his voicemail. I sent him a text asking that he call me right away. One can't easily explain a feeling in a text.

Randy usually answers texts quickly and particularly those coming from me. This time his response was faster than usual. It read as follows and left me worried: "Busy and can't talk. Don't do anything until you speak with me!"

Missy, what have you gotten me into? I wondered, as I placed the phone on my desk.

"What is it?" Missy asked, staring into my concerned face.

"God help us, I just don't know," I replied.

I walked to the window and looked into the sunny sky as if the answer could be found there. But it wasn't. Nor did it come from Randy when he phoned an hour later.

"I'm sorry, but I was in class," he apologized.

"OK, so what's up?" I asked, abruptly. "Your text scared me."

"It was meant to," Randy replied.

When he didn't immediately explain, I let the silence grow between us. Randy is great at clearing up science and math matters but explaining ordinary things can throw him. I waited until he collected his thoughts.

"I decrypted part of the file containing Odis' diary. His encryption was ingenious. The final key was choosing the correct photo from an array of twenty. He's definitely an above average hacker."

There was another pause during which I kept myself from screaming. Let Randy tell it his way, he'll get there eventually, I ordered myself.

"Before you can understand, I'll have to explain some things. Basically, math is the study of patterns to form hypotheses and discover relationships. Are you on speaker? Is Missy listening?"

"Yes, I replied, nodding toward her.

"Good. Well, by finding regularities in the data, we can predict what comes next. There are patterns in how nature and biology function, and in playing card games too.

"Now, some things are not what they seem but are illusions. Lines can cause an optical illusion. But the more data that you study and the more sophisticated is your math, the more accurate will be your predictions. Odis must be one curious guy."

"Like you," I interrupted, ignoring my dad's advice to never do so when a person's story is flowing.

"You could say that," Randy said, and I sensed the pride in his tone.

"So Odis discovered a pattern of dangerous events," Missy said, summarizing the conclusion that Randy seemed to be approaching.

"You sure could say that since it involved murder–and more," Randy replied.

His tone was, to make another of my bad puns, deadly serious.

Chapter 38

Both Missy and I felt stunned and didn't say anything for a while. Murder and the "more" of Randy's statement aren't everyday events. But Missy's question wasn't about those things.

"Is Odis alive?" she asked, in a slow, deliberate tone.

A hush enveloped the room as we awaited Randy's answer.

"Yes, I believe that he is," Randy said finally.

Missy broke down in tears and I placed my arm around her.

"Why did he disappear?" she asked, after regaining self-control.

"I don't know. Nothing in his diary refers to that but part of the file is corrupted and I haven't been able to clean it up. That's what I hope to do next.

"My sense is that he was trying to protect his family. He became a danger to an enemy, whoever they were. In his diary, he questions whether he'll survive. But he's so resourceful that I do believe he lives–somewhere."

Upon hearing these words, Missy again broke down. This time she didn't try to control her tears.

"I'll hang up. I have no more information," Randy said, recognizing that Missy needed me.

"My darling," I said softy.

"Love you," he said, and I replied "always,"

Other couples have their special words and these are ours.

After hanging up, I turned to Missy. She sobbed softly.

"I couldn't go on living if anything happens to Odis," she said earnestly, as if I must understand.

I didn't reply that she would soon be a mother, that her baby needed her, and that people survive loss. Though true, these words would have sounded trivial. Missy already knew the score.

But when Missy spoke, I recognized her strength and that she didn't need soothing words.

"If my baby is a boy his middle name will be Odis, and if it's a girl..."

"Odette?" I suggested.

"No, Cordelia," she said, firmly.

"Cordelia, from Shakespeare's play, *King Lear*?" I asked.

Cordelia was the favorite child of King Lear. She refused to express her love for her father in exchange for a third of his kingdom, feeling that this act would be unworthy of true love.

"No, the Cordelia who battles the supernatural in *Buffy the Vampire Slayer*," Missy replied, with the barest hint of a grin.

Chapter 39

After hearing news like that, things don't quickly return to normal. But we tried since there was nothing for us to do until we learned more from Randy. So we followed his advice to "do nothing," hoping to appear typical students.

Barnard College is not a good place for a mother. They state upfront that no child-care arrangements are available. Not limited child-care, not child-care is possible, but none.

Still, long before that need arose came Missy's issues of when to inform her parents of her pregnancy and where to give birth. With these, Missy did what most people do when they're uncertain. She put off her decisions.

I helped her as I had done with Hillary during her pregnancy: providing childbirth information and a shoulder to cry on when she needed it.

This wasn't as often as I had expected since Missy was sturdier than I had believed. She'll tell her parents, have a healthy baby, and we'll find Odis. These outcomes are what I hoped–and prayed for.

We had enrolled in the same classes in order to share homework chores. But this intention quickly fell by the wayside, being crushed by my desire to reduce Missy's stress. While she listened to music and relaxed, I did the homework for both of us. Still, we survived and thrived unlike some other students.

Two residents on our floor had already dropped out. One, after her noisy, ambulance attended, drug overdose; the second, like Odis, disappeared without a word. One day she was here and the next day she was gone. Even her roommate didn't know why or where. Like they say, shit happens.

What occurred next wasn't shit or unexpected. But it was unwelcome considering all that was happening. Despite her vow not to do so until Odis was found, Missy fell in love. With who you ask? Why with Artur of course.

Two days after they met, he appeared at our room bearing two gourmet vegetarian pizzas. This is the equivalent of flowers for us. Thereafter, college cafeteria meals became a rarity for Missy though not for me. You didn't really expect me to be a third wheel did you?

What did Artur think of Missy being pregnant? This isn't something that you tell a potential boyfriend on the first or even second date.

As weeks passed, Missy and Artur spent more time together. Her cheeks bloomed, and our double room turned into my single.

Were Missy and Artur practicing safe sex? Did Artur resemble the father of her child? Did Missy intend to deceive him? Some questions even a best friend doesn't ask and though Missy and I were "good friends" she hadn't yet joined my category of "best friends" like Erika and Hillary.

Chapter 40

I soon concluded that Missy was a survivor and stopped worrying about her. This decision was made easier by the fact that, apart from occasional classes, I now rarely saw her and when we met she spoke little.

What happened is what tends to happen when a girl finds her guy: their relationship pushes out all others. This, though most girls learn early on that while your boyfriend might leave you, your best girlfriends are your buddies forever.

We'll see how their relationship goes, I told myself, and threw myself into the classwork that I was doing for the two of us.

While I was beginning to love Barnard, Manhattan is expensive and my family's poverty crippled my off-campus activity. My mind returned to getting a part-time job. What skills did I have that were worth paying for? The Greenwich range instructor had described me as being a gifted pistol shooter but this wouldn't increase my employability in New York City.

People speak of the importance of networking when looking for a job. I introduced myself at dorm parties and hinted that I was looking for a job. It didn't help.

All of the parties that I attended were small and awkward or I might have picked the wrong night. From one girl I learned that the best night to party was

Thursday since most students didn't have classes on Friday. Unfortunately, I did.

I also learned that most partying was done over drinks in bars or a club. Both weren't possible for this poverty-stricken, non-drinking Mormon.

The solution to my problem came on a bulletin board notice: the Barnard Babysitting Agency had an upcoming orientation for "sitters looking for a job."

I went to their office in Elliott Hall, filled out the needed forms, and described my (paid) babysitting experience in Greenwich which included managing the babysitting service that Erika and I had set up. The next day I was sent for an interview to a prospective employer, the single parent of a seven-year-old boy.

Dr. Wilby, his parent, was an obstetrician who lived in an apartment house on Central Park West at 88th Street. I could have traveled there by bus or subway and chose the latter since it is faster. I left the subway at 86st Street and Broadway and walked several long blocks to the building.

There, I was announced by the doorman before taking the elevator to the 11th floor. I rang the apartment's bell and heard a woman's yell within. You're about to meet your boss, I told myself. I did.

Chapter 41

Dr. Wilby, Charlotte as she asked that I address her, looked as unlike a doctor as any woman that I could imagine. She was tall, nearly six feet in height, had long, flowing blond hair, blue eyes, small, perky breasts unrestrained by a bra, and a face that models would kill for.

She was stylishly dressed, according to those who follow clothing trends, in an unlined suede T-shirt and a suede wraparound skirt. "Suede is the current luxurious, but not ostentatious Jason Wu look" according to my dorm's fashion expert. "If you *must* ask the price, you can't afford it," she felt the need to tell me.

Charlotte's son, Tristan, was equally well-dressed despite the stain on his Star Wars jacket. Under it he wore a T-shirt with the words "Mommy's Angel". That's probably more prayer than fact, I thought. His first word to me was "No!" I smiled in response. Charlotte glared at her son. He got the hint and retreated to a corner of the room with his tablet.

"He's usually such a darling," Charlotte said, beaming a smile at me.

"No," her son yelled.

"Tell me about yourself. I'm not working today and have a glass of wine about now. Will you join me?" Charlotte asked.

"Thanks, but no. I'm Mormon and don't drink," I replied.

Since arriving at Barnard, I had stated this so often that I considered having "Another Mormon" tattooed on my arm to save time."

"I'm Mormon too but occasionally feel the need for something to help me relax. Wine is far less dangerous than smoking."

I nodded my understanding. There had been times when I needed a drink too. I spoke my prepared introduction as the Barnard Babysitting Service had advised.

"I come from Greenwich and am in my first year at Barnard. My father is a lawyer and my mother was a teacher. I have three sisters. My older sister is a film student at NYU. In Greenwich, I and a friend ran a babysitting service. It was similar to Barnard's except that we used high school babysitters. I made a list of the phone numbers of my parents and my doctor and people in town who can vouch for me."

I gave her the sheet with these numbers.

After glancing over it, she ordered her son, "Tristan, go to your room."

He ignored her, being absorbed in his video game.

"*Tristan, go to your room. Mommy wants to speak with the nice lady alone,*" Charlotte repeated, more loudly.

Tristan got up, glared at his mother as if to say, I'm doing this because I want to and not because you're ordering me to, and left.

"Tristan doesn't have a father. Maybe that's why he can be like this," Charlotte said.

"You're divorced?" I asked.

"No. I never married but always wanted a child. Eight years ago I realized that I was getting on and if I wanted a child I'd better get busy. I couldn't trust my lover to be a good father so I used a sperm donor. Tristan has excellent genes. He should be grateful to me for at least that."

"Kids aren't easy to deal with. I'm sure that you're a great mother," I said.

My tone had been reassuring even as I realized the absurdity of a teenager telling this to a woman twice her age.

"No. I love being a doctor and a good mother makes her kids her priority. I keep Tristan clothed and fed and read with him daily—he's a good reader—and make play dates for him with other up-and-coming kids. But to be honest, I'm not the best mother and I know it."

I didn't reply. There was nothing tactful that I could say.

Chapter 42

Charlotte lay the sheet of paper containing the phone numbers that I had given her on the coffee table.

"I already received these from the Babysitting Service and have checked with several of your references. All have the highest opinion of you so we needn't spend more time on that," Charlotte said.

"Both Tristan and I have busy schedules that often conflict. He's in school from 8:30AM to 3:00PM and attends an after-school program until 6:00PM. I occasionally have night calls as do all obstetricians. I can't be sure when I'll be home. There is a spare bedroom if you must stay overnight, and I'll open an Uber account for you to taxi here from school and back.

"You can do your homework while Tristan sleeps. I'll pay you double for your hours after 8PM and for your travel time both ways. How does that sound?"

"That's exceptionally generous," I replied, already calculating how much money I would earn.

"Yes, it is, but I've found that paying well is cheaper in the long run," Charlotte said, with a small smile.

Then she familiarized me with the apartment. It had the high ceilings, large rooms, and plaster wall paneling characteristic of eighty-year-old structures.

Tristan's room was brightly colored in white and blue. Its desk, secretarial chair, and desktop computer seemed out of place in a seven-year-old's room. But maybe not for this child, I thought. When we entered, Tristan lay on his bed reading a thick, obviously adult book. He didn't look up and we quickly left.

"What's he reading?" I asked Charlotte, after she closed the door.

"It looks like one of my medical texts," she said.

I stared and she added, "He's very bright."

The spare bedroom was small but contained the essentials: a double bed, a tiny bedside table on the far side where the angled wall was difficult to utilize, and a chair doubling as another bedside table to give the room a more spacious feel. This room also had a white/blue color scheme along with a deep bay window and plants. Each bedroom had its own bathroom, unlike the communal facilities of my dorm.

"It's lovely," I said, as the tour ended, and we sat in plush club chairs beside the fireplace in the living room.

"It'll be comfortable. Feel free to ask if you ever feel the need for something for you or Tristan. I may not be the best mother but he is my life and I'll do anything for him," Charlotte said, brushing away tears.

Her discomfort was obvious and I looked away as Charlotte changed the subject.

"Are you religious?" she asked, abruptly.

"That depends how you mean. My family attends church every Sunday but they're flexible. If they weren't,

I wouldn't have been allowed to date my boyfriend since we were thirteen. Particularly since his family isn't Mormon or even religious. Missy, my roommate, is Mormon too. We've been to the new West Side Temple, but mostly to make social contacts. Her father is a bishop but Missy is...well...her boyfriend is probably an atheist," I said.

"How do you know that?"

"His father is Russia's military attaché. I doubt that they're religious," I said.

I had been disturbed by her question. Religion has *nothing* to do with babysitting!

Charlotte sensed my uneasiness.

"I don't care what religion you are. I was just thinking that since you're Mormon and I'm a lapsed one, you could take Tristan to the Church on occasional Sundays when I'm working. I've read that it's beautiful and he might find it interesting.

"Incidentally, I've never had Tristan baptized. This is another reason why my family has little to do with us. Tristan can choose whatever religion he wants–or no religion–when he's an adult. We're both individualistic."

I smiled, nodded, and now felt completely at home.

Chapter 43

A minute later, Charlotte got a call about a medical emergency and my babysitting began that afternoon. She re-introduced me to Tristan, changed her clothes, and left. I had expected for him to make a scene about his mother leaving but he didn't. I sat beside his bed and awaited a reaction. Tristan remained engrossed in his book, either from interest or to give me the cold shoulder. But I felt completely at home. When my mother gets furious with me she stops talking to me.

"I'm getting juice for myself. Do you want anything?" I asked, in my sweetest tone.

"Yes, for you to go home!" he said, angrily.

"I'll get a juice for you too," I replied, and then did.

I placed the juice on his night table, seated myself on the desk chair, and scanned an issue of the *Journal of the American Medical Association* that I had picked up from the kitchen counter.

"What are you studying?" Tristan asked, in a friendly manner.

I looked up quickly, being surprised by his tone.

"I'm not sure. I love to write and am taking an English class but also science and math classes. The usual that First Year students take at Barnard," I replied.

Tristan said nothing as he digested these facts.

"How do you like your school?" I asked.

"I don't. It's boring."

"What will you be doing next summer?" I asked.

"You'll have to ask Charlotte. She makes all the decisions around here."

I was surprised that Tristan referred to his mother by her first name but, as I had long before learned, families make their own rules.

"Do you want to play a game?" I asked.

"Chess," he replied, and that's what we did.

From my experiences with young kids, I knew that it's not unusual for them to play games in a babyish fashion: cheating, and playing by their own rules. Tristan surprised me by playing chess like an adult, and well too. He beat me in less time than I feel comfortable admitting. It was while we were playing that he asked an odd question.

"Do you have a father?"

"Everyone has a father. Your father doesn't live with you, just like with many children," I replied softly, having a sense of where he was going with his question.

There was a period of silence while Tristan thought.

"I'll never know my father," he said.

"Probably not but he gave you good things: you're healthy and very smart," I said.

Margaret of Greenwich

The silence lengthened as he opened and drank from the juice box that I had brought him.

Chapter 44

My first day on the job turned out to be my first night at it too. And despite my initial worry, caring for Tristan presented no difficulty. He ate what I prepared, showered and got into his pajamas when I suggested, and amused himself with his books and video games.

This left me a bit disappointed. I had prepared myself to be his occasional mother but he related to me as a friend or an older sister.

So after calling and leaving a message for Missy that I might be out all night, I did our homework. Her homework had become her relationship with Artur and keeping herself healthy.

After tiring of doing homework, I considered phoning Randy but hesitated. I didn't want to become one of those nags that everyone hates. At nine I checked that Tristan was asleep and he was. On his bed lay the book that he had been reading: Sigmund Freud's, *The Interpretation of Dreams*.

This is *some* child that I'm babysitting, I thought, as I removed the book from his bed and placed it on the night table. I plugged in the Disney night light before turning off the bedside lamp and tiptoeing from the room.

I left the door of Tristan's room open and it was good that I did. An hour later, I heard him screaming for Charlotte and I rushed to his room. He was sobbing and looked the helpless, vulnerable child that all seven-year-olds are.

"What's wrong?" I asked, after going to his bed and hugging him.

"Dream," he said, in a breathless voice.

"Do you want to tell me about it?" I asked, and he shook his head.

"OK. How about some juice?" I asked.

I knew from my earlier babysitting that nothing reduces a child's upset more quickly than eating.

I interpreted Tristan's silence as "yes" and went to the kitchen. There, I found apple, orange, and berry juice boxes. I chose the apple juice having learned that, for whatever reason, young children tend to prefer it.

Back at Tristan's side, I opened the juice box and inserted the straw. I didn't doubt that he could do it for himself but I sensed that he needed mothering after his cry for Charlotte.

Just as I had calmed him down and left his room, Charlotte arrived home. She looked exhausted.

"How did it go?" she asked, in a tired voice.

"Fine. He's a *wonderful* child. There were no problems," I replied.

"His history with babysitters isn't happy. You were a good choice," Charlotte said.

Chapter 45

Charlotte set up the Uber account on my IPhone and showed me how to call for a ride. The charge would be billed to her credit card.

"Feel free to use it around the City. Few of Tristan's babysitters have lasted more than one evening. Whether it's because of mine or his father's genes I won't try to guess. I wasn't the easiest child either."

I smiled and settled for saying "Thank you." Once again, there was nothing tactful for me to say.

The Uber driver came quickly, his car was spotless, and he drove as quickly and safely as one can in Manhattan traffic. He wasn't talkative and we both relaxed with the lilting jazz from his CD.

I felt exhausted and tumbling into bed was my most immediate thought. But this was not to be. Soon after entering the dorm, I was corralled by students into the Lounge. There, girls sat spellbound, listening to advice from two expensively dressed men.

Barnard drama is little different from high school drama and the most important issues are often the same. That evening's presentations concerned hair and boobs: *How to Turn Your Skin Around,* and *How to Gain Perky Breasts Without Going the Implant Route.*

Though my eyes occasionally drifted shut, I tried to remember what was advised. What woman wouldn't when the advice was coming from doctors?

The girls stared open-mouthed as the dermatologist spoke. His suggested routine was so extensive that I'd sooner lose Randy than go through it daily. It involved the morning use of a cleanser, hyaluronic acid serum, retinol serum, and a moisturizer with sunscreen and growth factors. The nightly use of a cleanser, retinol eye cream and face cream, and a moisturizer with growth factors. Additionally, a sheet mask with Vitamin E was to be used twice a week.

"This may seem like a lot but you'll feel its worth as your skin becomes smoother and more radiant," the doctor said.

I passed on his product coupons, feeling too young for such worries.

"The current trend in breast surgery isn't for what you've never had but for what you've *lost!*" the other doctor, a plastic surgeon, said emphatically.

She used a PowerPoint demonstration to distinguish traditional breast lift from the newest procedures: *Breast Lift With Mesh Reinforcement*, and *Breast Lift With Fat Injections*.

"Twenty-five percent of breast-lift patients in 2013 were between the ages of nineteen and thirty-four. They now feel more feminine, more comfortable in clothing, a bathing suit, and when naked," she added, to her increasingly nervous listeners.

One more year and I fall apart, I thought, sorrowfully.

Margaret of Greenwich

I left before the Q&A and went to my room. A man stood leaning against the door. He straightened at my approach.

"Can we talk alone for a few minutes?" Artur asked.

Chapter 46

Though Artur's request was reasonable, it took me a moment to realize who was standing at my door and to respond. I had picked up a sheet describing the next doctor talk. This one was entitled "The Five Most Embarrassing Sex Questions—Answered" and my mind had been on that. *Would* my vagina be noticeably bigger after having a child? I could only worry.

So to change from thought of my vagina to whether it was OK for me to speak with Missy's boyfriend without her being present took thinking. I resolved this conflict by telling myself that Artur is my relative, a courtesy cousin insofar as Vladimir is a courtesy father. This isn't logical but it made me feel better.

"Sure, where's Missy?" I asked Artur, as soon as I regained proper focus.

"We had a bit of an argument and she's walking it off."

"Do you *really* want to tell me about it?" I asked, now feeling hesitant.

"Yes, maybe you can explain what happened. I might have missed something since my English isn't good."

"You speak it fine," I said, supportively.

"I can miss slang and maybe that's what happened."

"What happened?"

"I asked if she was on the pill. Is this something American girls don't talk about?"

Uh Oh, I thought. Has Missy told him that she's pregnant? What should I reply? I wondered.

To give myself time to think, I invited Artur in. Even before the door had closed, I decided that it was best for me to say nothing. It's hard to give good advice when one hasn't heard both sides of a quarrel. Their dispute may have related to Artur's question or not. The only certainty was that if he had asked that question, he must be unaware that Missy is pregnant.

Artur was drinking from the juice box that I had given him. This came from my notion that since food calms an upset kid, it might have the same effect on a wounded lover.

"How were things going with Missy before you raised the question?" I asked.

"She seemed upset all evening but when I asked if she was OK she said that she was fine. She just sat and knitted."

I spoke quickly, not wanting Artur to wonder what Missy was knitting.

"Artur, Missy is sometimes unhappy with her family and it hits her at times. Then, she becomes quiet and I leave her alone. She comes out of it in a while and is OK. It's probably best not to question her. You can never be sure what'll arouse a bad memory."

"Thank you. You're a good friend to Missy and I'm glad you're my cousin. I'll do as you say."

I smiled and Artur smiled and left.

Missy, what are you doing? I asked myself. I undressed and got into bed. Despite feeling exhausted, I was unable to sleep.

Chapter 47

I came right to the point when Missy returned an hour later.

"You haven't told him," I said.

My tone wasn't accusatory but matter of fact, as was her reply.

"No."

"When do you plan to?" I asked.

"Why do you want to know?"

Like my lawyer-dad said, a person who answers a question with a question is neither a good witness nor a good liar.

"Because I've been pulled into it. Artur is upset and just left. He wanted to know why his question whether you're on the pill so upset you."

"What did you say?"

"That you're sad about your family and on some days anything will set you off. What else could I say?"

"Thanks."

"He must find out eventually," I said softly.

I wasn't angry. No girl should be when her friend is dealing with Missy's situation. When should a girl tell her boyfriend about a potentially game changing fact in their relationship?

"I'm going to sleep," Missy said, and that's what we both did.

The next day we returned to our student routine. This had a calming effect and Missy's mood was brighter. Artur sent us a text inviting the two of us to lunch that day. We met at a health food restaurant on Broadway and were glad of the change. The dining hall's vegetarian choices are limited and rarely change.

I wondered why Artur had invited me since I would be an obvious third wheel. I concluded that he felt my calming presence would be needed but it wasn't. I told stories about Greenwich, Missy spoke of her high school cheerleading, and Artur spoke of his future.

"Will you return to Russia after graduating?" Missy asked.

Though her tone was casual, we both knew that her interest was anything but that.

"I don't know. My father is a diplomat and the government has a rule that they can't stay in one setting for more than four years. He might want me to attend a Russian medical school. I have just a student visa here," Artur replied.

"What do you want to do?" I asked.

"I want to stay. My dad might be able to get an extension. He has good contacts in Moscow."

Missy's eyes watered and I knew what she was thinking: first, I lose Odis and now Artur.

"Four years is a long way off. Much can happen in that time," I said.

And in seven months too, I thought.

Chapter 48

During my first year at Barnard we came to think of events as being in one of two categories: "BB" or "AB." The happenings that came before or after the blackout.

The power failure wasn't total, it affecting only the West side of Manhattan north of 110th Street. By twist of fate, though few believed it, this is also one of the poorer sections of the City.

The blackout began early on a Wednesday evening and lasted until nearly 7PM the following day. Nowadays everyone is so used to having electricity that we tend to forget how vital it is until it is gone.

We first considered the event a momentary outage. These are common and why computer backup batteries are sold. But text messages quickly arrived from the college informing us what had happened. Student could, if they wished, walk several blocks to St. Luke's hospital and remain there until the emergency was over. The hospital has generators to provide essential services. Police, aided by the college's private security guards, would patrol the area to insure safety.

While the dorm bathrooms functioned, our rations were limited: two bags of organic corn chips, six juice boxes of orange juice, and three bananas.

We gathered our supplies. The elevators weren't working so we walked down the stairs to the TV lounge on the first floor. There was no TV but we didn't want to be alone.

There, students happily milled about since the blackout was the best possible reason for missing a class deadline. Some had flashlights while others used the flashlight app on their phone or tablet. Couples were locked in embraces–and more–in corners. Anonymity brings many things.

My phone rang. It's probably my parents who heard about the blackout and are checking to see that I'm OK, I instantly thought, but it wasn't.

"I just got a call from the hospital. One of my patients is going into labor. Can you come over now? We have electricity and Wi-Fi. I'll leave the password so you can do your homework," Charlotte said, in a breathless voice.

"OK, but Uber could be expensive. Their fares are based on demand and taxies are very in demand now," I said.

"Don't worry about that. You might have to stay over so bring some things," Charlotte replied.

"Can I bring my roommate—a girl?" I asked.

"As long as you get here quickly," Charlotte replied, before hanging up.

I told Missy that we would be going to an apartment with lights and Wi-Fi.

"Great! Whose apartment is it?" she asked.

"Hopefully, your future obstetrician's," I replied, as I led her to get our things.

Chapter 49

Missy didn't speak again until we were in the taxi.

"Is the obstetrician the mother that you're babysitting for?" she asked.

"Yes, and she's a good doctor if her expensive apartment means anything. She's also single and would be sympathetic to your situation."

"I don't *need* sympathy. What did you tell her about me?" Missy asked, with a flash of anger.

"Nothing! But you have no money and will need an obstetrician and she could be it," I replied.

Missy accepted this, and remained silent until reaching Charlotte's apartment.

Charlotte gave us a smile but was in a rush. She hollered back from the doorway, "Ask Tristan what he wants for supper," and was gone.

Tristan was reading in his room when I introduced him to Missy. After briefly staring at her, his question startled us and we were momentarily speechless.

"Are you having a baby?" Tristan asked.

Though he had addressed Missy, I answered first, using the well-worn technique of putting off having to reply to one question by asking another.

"What makes you think that?" I asked.

"Her stomach," Tristan replied, before returning to his medical text.

"What would you like for dinner?" I asked, being glad that the topic of Missy's belly had lost interest for him.

"Salmon cakes and spaghetti," Tristan replied, after several moments of thought. "It's in the freezer," he added helpfully.

Being an awful cook, I sighed with relief.

Missy turned toward me when we reached the kitchen.

"That boy is astonishing," she said, wide-eyed.

"He's the product of his mother's egg and well-chosen sperm. Nobody doubts that he's a genius," I said.

Would Tristan share his suspicion about Missy with his mother? I asked myself, before reassuring myself with a simple thought. What if he does? She's a doctor.

Chapter 50

While eating our microwaved meal, Tristan readily answered our questions. At first with just a few words but then more extensively.

He said that he liked to read and to play chess. His love for TV cartoon shows surprised me since I had expected him to have adult tastes here too. Still, he was only seven-years-old and his current worry was being bullied at school.

"I told the teacher and she did nothing," he said sadly.

"How do they bully you?" Missy asked.

"They call me 'geek' and 'fag' and say that I can't be a man since I don't have a father. And what can I do about that?"

"How old are they?" I asked.

"They're older, in seventh grade."

"The idiots. Did you tell your mom?" I asked, angrily.

"Yes. She said to ignore them, that words can't kill you. Then she went to work."

"Words won't kill you but they *can* hurt," I said sympathetically.

Missy nodded agreement.

A babysitter's only task is to keep a child healthy and happy until their parent returns home. I knew what I was doing wasn't right. But I felt that if Charlotte didn't help Tristan to battle the bullies then I had to. He was too young to learn the combat moves that I knew. My suggested squelch would have to be enough and I thought that it would be.

"I know something that you could say when those boys bother you again," I said, moving my head closer to Tristan's. "Say that they're mad because their mom is your ho. Can you remember that?"

Tristan looked puzzled before he burst out laughing.

"You're just mad because your mom's my ho!" he repeated.

"Just like that. I don't think they'll bother you again," I said, confidently.

Tristan's gloom suddenly lifted. Until his bedtime, he chose the show that we would watch: an old Nickelodeon teen soap opera, *Fifteen,* that he had found on Netflix. It is an easy to understand show though more than a little melodramatic. Matt is athlete and alcoholic. His girlfriend, Ashley, is sweet, charming, and gets sent to another school. Both begin dating others and you can imagine the rest.

"TV is probably where Tristan learned about whores,'" Missy said, when we were alone.

"I'd hate to think that he has nothing left to learn," I replied.

"But how could he have known I'm pregnant?" Missy asked.

"That doesn't take a genius. Look sideways in a mirror. You're starting to show," I replied.

Chapter 51

Charlotte didn't get home until after 3AM. Electricity wasn't restored on campus until late the next morning. We stayed at her apartment that night and until lunchtime the following day.

That morning, Charlotte had paperwork to do so Missy and I walked Tristan to school with each of us holding one of his hands. Before parting at the door, he turned to us, grinned, and whispered, "Your mom is my ho!"

"*Good boy*," I said.

I smiled and kissed him on the forehead. Missy kissed him goodbye too. Tristan's family is expanding, I thought.

Upon our return to the apartment, Charlotte looked up from the paper-strewn dining room table where she had been working. She expressed the same observation about Missy that Tristan had: "You're pregnant." It wasn't a question but a statement. Pregnancy is her business.

"Yes," Missy answered simply.

"Third month?" Charlotte asked and Missy nodded.

"Sit," Charlotte ordered us.

We obeyed, taking chairs opposite her at the table.

"What are you going to do?" Charlotte asked.

"I'm going to have the baby," Missy replied.

"*OK*," Charlotte said slowly, drawing out the syllables.

"Do your parents know?"

"Not yet."

"Does the father know?"

"No. He's dead."

Charlotte's eyes widened. I just listened, being a third party to their conversation.

"What about school? Pregnant students aren't exactly Barnard's style," Charlotte asked.

"I don't want to drop out but haven't figured that part out yet. They might throw me out," Missy replied.

"Are you on scholarship?"

"No," Missy replied.

"I'm no lawyer but I think that it would be hard for the administration to expel you just for being pregnant. They wouldn't want a lawsuit and the resulting nasty publicity, particularly at a woman's college. What happened to the father? Was he a soldier?"

Missy's mouth opened. She swallowed hard but no words came out. She began sobbing. I hadn't intended to say anything but Missy needed Charlotte as an ally. There's only so much help that a teenager can give. So although the facts that Missy shared had been told to me in confidence, I described her predicament to Charlotte. Her response indicated that I hadn't made a mistake.

"The baby's father was a guidance counselor in her school. Missy's brother disappeared ten years ago and only she believes him alive. She needed a friend and the counselor took advantage of her and other students too. He either ran away or killed himself when he feared being arrested. He left a suicide note but they never found a body."

Charlotte looked out the window thoughtfully before turning toward Missy.

"You need a doctor. Will you accept me as your doctor?" Charlotte asked.

Missy didn't look up. She softly murmured, "thank you."

"After your child is born you'll need a place to stay. No matter how flexible Barnard is, I can't see them permitting an infant to live in the dorm. Would you consider staying here? Tristan has been plaguing me to have another child but him and my medical work is all that I can deal with. It would be good for him if you and your child lived here."

Again, Missy nodded.

"So now everything is fine," Charlotte said, and smiled.

Missy dried her eyes. She tried to return Charlotte's smile but only mine was real.

Chapter 52

When we returned to the dorm there was a party in progress. It was if everyone was overjoyed to have survived though the blackout had been nothing compared with the typical disaster.

We smiled, and walked quickly to our room.

"Do I really show?" Missy asked, peering at her body sideways in the mirror.

"Well, you've just received the opinion of two experts."

"I wouldn't consider Tristan an expert."

"No, but he is a genius and he was right," I replied.

I was expecting this question and had been thinking about it. Hillary had faced the same situation, and there had been times in my life when disguise was important.

"Starting now, you'll have to eat for the two of you but sneak in the extras when we're alone in the lunchroom. Wear a billowy top but slim below, and accessories that cause people to look at them rather than at your body. Also, wear different makeup to keep people guessing and throw on a scarf for camouflage. This'll work for a few months."

"What then?" Missy asked.

"No one can predict the future. Then we deal with things as they come," I said.

Missy nodded and lay down to nap. It had been an exhausting two days. While she napped I did our homework. Then I called Randy and told him about the blackout.

"I heard about it. How was it?" he asked.

"Not bad. The doctor that I'm babysitting for was called in to work so Missy and I spent the night in her apartment with lights and Wi-Fi. She had opened an Uber account for me and we taxied there."

"How is the child?"

"He's seven and a total delight. I'm honing my mothering skills."

Randy didn't immediately reply. We were both virgins and sex wasn't easy for him to talk about even indirectly. He changed the subject.

"I've decrypted more of Odis' diary. He was cautious and used different codes in different parts. I haven't gotten to the last part yet."

"What do you think was going on?" I asked.

"I don't yet know. He uses coded initials and phrases, the most important seeming to be small 'g' capital 'B' capital 'M' and 'sea breeze.' One group seems involved in just about everything criminal: racketeering, drug trafficking, loan sharking, robbery, and the murder of members of 'AC.' I don't yet know what that is. It's a puzzle."

"A puzzle," I repeated. "How are *you*? Are you taking care of yourself?"

"I try," Randy said, casually.

His tone made me nervous though Randy has always been healthy.

"Randy!" I said, sternly.

"Yes, mama, I'm taking care of myself. And you take care of yourself too. Love you."

"Always," I said, these words being our usual signing-off custom.

I looked toward Missy after hanging up the phone. I decided not to tell her Randy's latest information. She had enough worries.

Chapter 53

Campus life returned to normal the day after the blackout ended. Missy followed my advice about dress, and I made sure that she never sat alone in the cafeteria lest uncomfortable questions be asked.

Yet even were Missy alone she likely wouldn't have been bothered for we hadn't yet made friends. Being vegetarians that didn't smoke or drink or use drugs, we might have been judged too different. It may also be that we were too involved with our own problems to appear concerned with those of others.

Charlotte accepted an additional OB/GYN appointment at Lenox Hill Hospital, Manhattan's preferred birthing center for wealthy parents. As her workload increased, I spent more time with Tristan and Missy accompanied me. She became increasingly nervous as her pregnancy advanced. Being in a doctor's apartment comforted her even if the doctor wasn't there.

But Tristan was there and seeing Missy's distress changed him. Though he might be nasty to me, he was always friendly and respectful to Missy. *She* held his brother or sister. This, though they remain unrelated no matter how many days we slept in the bedroom adjoining his.

Classes went well and I didn't mind doing most of our homework. There had been many times in my life when others helped me and that is what friends are for.

Missy was grateful. When she hinted at my becoming her child's godparent, I smiled but didn't reply. I was already godparent to Hillary's daughter. Is there a limit to this role for a teenager? I wondered.

Looking back, all in all, the early months of Missy's pregnancy was a peaceful time. The proverbial calm before the storm, like the "phony war" before the Nazis invaded Western Europe in 1940. For our English class we were reading old books written by refugees. It was not a happy period.

Randy had advised us to keep a low profile since Odis' activities could be arousing a hornet's nest. We tried but, as has been said, man proposes and God disposes.

As with all pregnant women, Missy's outlook would quickly become gloomy. To lift her mood, Artur and I took her to a movie that we hoped would help. It was an old film, *Sydney White*, and was being shown at the Museum of Modern Art.

The movie is about a poor girl, Sydney White, who wins a college scholarship. She hopes to follow in the sorority footsteps of her mother who died when Sydney was four. After realizing that sorority life isn't for her, she moves out of the group's house into The Vortex, a community of losers, and runs for Student Body President. She wants to change campus attitudes about what is important.

Though the lines aren't great ("I'm the last person you want to mess with." "No. You're the first."), the movie lifted Missy's spirit. She smiled as we walked to the subway.

Minutes later, none of us were smiling.

Chapter 54

"Should we take the subway or bus?"

I had asked this familiar question as we left MOMA, which is what New Yorkers call the Museum of Modern Art on West 53rd Street. Traveling there from the Barnard campus can be done by subway or bus.

"Subway," Missy said.

Travel by subway was new for Missy. Despite the crowds, for her it was an adventure not a chore.

We walked to the Columbus Circle station on West 59th Street. There, we waited for the local Broadway train. It would take us to the 116th Street campus station.

While we chatted about the movie, three men in their early twenties walked down the platform. One grabbed a teenager's cap and punched him when he protested. Another grabbed a woman's purse. She screamed and was knocked to the ground. She lay still either from shock or injury.

As they approached, Artur moved in front of us and took a heavy, antique, three-sided ruler from his backpack. It was used in his bioengineering class. I remembered Missy's pistol, then that she had stopped carrying it after learning of her pregnancy.

A mugger stationed himself before us as the others approached.

"Does this hold an iPad?" he asked, leaning toward Missy's large purse.

At that moment, Artur struck. He smashed the ruler into the thief's throat and viciously kicked him in the groin as he went down. Then Artur rushed the other robbers, smashing one man's nose with the ruler and, as blood spurted, striking him again on the side of his head. As he fell, the third man turned and ran down the platform. Artur leaped after and tackled him, banging his head onto the concrete floor.

Artur then stood and looked around, as if making plans to deal with another assailant. When he saw that there weren't any, he rejoined us.

"Are you alright?" he asked calmly. He seemed to have hardly broken a sweat.

Loud cheers and handclapping erupted amongst the bystanders on the platform. They surrounded us as the police arrived and the circus began.

Officers took names, addresses, and statements. The muggers were arrested, and the injured woman was treated and taken to an ER. There were smiles all around as we boarded the train.

An onlooker had given the first arriving reporter a cell phone video of Artur's actions. It played repeatedly on the late evening news. By morning the film had gone viral and Artur's heroism was broadcast internationally. One newspaper's headline read, "Russian Diplomat's Son Saves Passengers From Muggers On NYC Subway."

There was a more restrained headline in the *Columbia Daily Spectator*, the student newspaper.

When a reporter asked Artur where he had learned to fight so well, Artur credited his father's instruction in self-defense.

Randy called me early the next morning.

"You probably won't take my advice after we're married either," he said.

"Huh?" I responded, to what must be the strangest marriage proposal ever.

"About keeping a low profile."

"Well, it wasn't as if we *chose* to be attacked," I replied, a bit angrily.

"I was just teasing. How are you?"

"Fine. Artur was astonishing."

"He said that he learned self-defense from his father. He must have some father."

"Yes, he does."

"He's a diplomat."

"Yes," I said simply, not adding what I knew about him.

Ivan, Artur's father, was also a trained killer. A year before, he had saved my life in London.

Chapter 55

Artur's celebrity turned him and Missy into *the* couple on campus. His photo had gone viral after the subway incident and E-mails from girls with ravenous, semi-naked bodies arrived regularly. But this didn't affect his relationship with Missy. Artur had apparently inherited both his father's good lucks and good thinking. Missy would be best for the long haul and who could say about these strangers.

The excitement wore down as exams approached. Grades were important to students, unlike crime which mostly occurred in the poorer areas of Manhattan. My time was spent studying, watching that Missy took care of herself, and babysitting Tristan. Because of Charlotte's increased work schedule, this had become nearly a full-time job. Nearly all of our exams were take-home and I mostly did Missy's too.

Yet even with all this going on, I still found time to speak with Randy over Skype daily and with my family every other day. He was successful at Yale but unhappy at our separation and this kept me content.

Over the years I had gradually concluded that life should be a series of adventures launched from a secure base. My secure base had been my family and this remained intact. Family is all that we have and one should try to keep it together. So, as people say, things could have been worse.

Margaret of Greenwich

A week before exams, Missy told Artur everything: her brother's disappearance, her affair with the school counselor who had vanished and was now presumed dead, and being pregnant. She had no choice if they weren't to stop having sex. Despite his great looks, Artur must have been inexperienced with women not to have noticed Missy's pregnancy, I thought.

According to Missy, the only change in Artur was that he became more loving. Vladimir repeatedly tells me that family is central for Russians. Artur might have viewed him and Missy and her baby as being a real family even if the baby wasn't his. Or he may have felt the need to have a mother in his life. Who knows? Being sure about anyone's behavior is beyond me.

Tristan approved of Artur as much as any seven-year-old can. Artur is a much better chess player than Missy or me and Tristan enjoyed the challenge. He also liked having a man in his life.

Thus, the five of us became another of today's atypical families: Charlotte mothered us while I and Missy and Artur became Tristan's older siblings who amused him and taught him adult skills. This might sound weird but it did work.

A popular saying is that all good things must end and we feared that they soon would. With the close of the semester, Missy's family, Artur's family, my family, and Randy planned to visit us and tour New York City. If you doubt that the City has become the vacation capital of the world, walk along the packed sidewalks of 42nd Street.

Artur's parents were broadminded but I worried about Missy's father. Being a Mormon bishop, he would expect to visit his virginal–not pregnant–daughter.

Chapter 56

"Parents automatically try to fix a problem and that often makes it worse," Missy said, as their visit approached.

"That's how parents are. They call their kids babyish but scream when they want to do things on their own," I replied.

Missy's fear was gone, replaced by the steely maternal conviction that pregnancy brings.

"I *won't* put my child up for adoption!" Missy insisted.

"No," I said, not supporting that decision but of her right to choose.

"I know that my parents will blame themselves and feel guilty though the affair was my fault."

"You can't say that. You were a child. What he did was criminal!" I insisted.

"*Yes*, it was a crime and shouldn't have happened but it didn't destroy me. Odis' disappearance did and Jerry pulled me from the paralysis that had taken over my life. I regained hope, and learned that I could love.

"Jerry being a monster doesn't change that fact and I now have Artur. I had been lost but sometimes getting lost is the only way to find what you didn't know you were looking for."

I didn't reply. This outpouring of words was unusual for Missy. Whether it reflected her nervousness or certainty I wasn't sure.

"How can I help?" I asked.

We had been speaking while preparing lunch for Tristan in Charlotte's kitchen. He was busy constructing a project with his new Raspberry Pi chip. This is a low-cost, credit sized computer that plugs into a monitor or TV and uses a standard keyboard and mouse. It's designed to help kids learn programming.

The chip can do everything that a desktop computer can do from browsing the internet to playing games. Projects like a weather station or a tweeting bird house with an infra-red camera can also be embarked on.

After its purchase, we rarely saw Tristan apart from meals. I occasionally feared what he might be building in his room but comforted myself with the thought that Einstein's parents might have had the same worry and his life certainly turned out OK.

"You can't help me more than you are. I'll have to deal with my parents on my own," Missy said, after moments of thinking.

"Well, maybe it won't be too bad," I said, in an optimistic tone.

Missy made a sheepish smile and shook her head.

"No, it'll be downright awful," she replied.

Chapter 57

Vladimir said that even atheists pray when something seems hopeless. And that, if wounded, they cry for their mother, not their father.

Despite Missy's show of courage, I could see that she was upset and so did Charlotte when she returned home. Upon learning what was bothering Missy, Charlotte told us a children's story, *The Little Prince*, that she had recently read to Tristan.

"A prince has only one rose and two volcanoes on his planet. He loves his rose so much that he builds a fence around it to keep it from being destroyed by insects. He is sure to water it daily.

"One day he is taken in a space ship to Earth and there he sees many roses. He first thinks that he was foolish to place a fence around his rose since there are so many roses on Earth. But then he realizes that while he doesn't love the Earth roses, he does love his rose. Not for its beauty but because he has watered it and cared for it and it is his.

"A child is the flower of their parents. They love their child because they have cared for them and because they are theirs. Parents do not desert them because they are imperfect. But whatever happens, you will always have a home with me and Tristan," Charlotte said.

Then Missy cried and I cried and all seemed well and we called Tristan for lunch. He couldn't stop talking about his latest Raspberry Pi project: a boxy, handheld gaming device running the old-fashioned Super Mario World for Super Nintendo.

Tristan's hobby kept him busy for the rest of the afternoon while Charlotte told us stories of her disastrous dating experiences, and how she knew when a relationship was over.

Charlotte had once noticed an unauthorized charge on her credit card statement for eighty-six dollars. Upon calling the store, she learned that her live-in boyfriend had used her card to send roses to "Marilyn."

Another boyfriend sent her a note asking that she return a paperback book he had lent her. He enclosed a stamped, self-addressed envelope to mail it in.

A third boyfriend had described her contribution to their live-in relationship as "rent." "We no longer kissed but went straight to sex and I realized that the best thing we had were memories."

"That was when I began searching for a sperm donor," Charlotte said.

Missy and I looked at each other and we both had the same thought: as difficult as our lives were, they could be worse.

Chapter 58

"Are you still looking for a husband?" Missy asked Charlotte.

We were relaxing in the living room, nibbling Pepperidge Farm Milano cookies and lemon sorbet, admittedly not the healthiest snacks.

It was so long before Charlotte answered that I wondered if she would. But her situation was complex. Tristan was a rare child and would not be the favored step-son for many men.

"I don't know. I do want a man in my life but I'm a mother. Tristan comes first, and my medical work is important too. Could I care for a man—be there for him— as much as I am for Tristan?

"How would Tristan relate to a stranger entering our family? He gets along well with you but views you like older sisters, not a parent. But Tristan will be off to college in ten years, and I'll be alone."

"What kind of man would you like?" I asked.

"From your mouth to the ears of God," Charlotte said, smiling before she became serious.

"When I was much younger I wanted someone who was handsome and wealthy. Those things aren't important to me now. What is crucial is that he help me become who I could be.

"When I was an intern, I had a patient who survived a terrible accident. Afterward, she was visited by two boyfriends. One brought her flowers and was sympathetic; the other asked how long she would stay in bed feeling sorry for herself. When he left, the woman became angry and insisted that she begin her physical therapy. I know which man loved her more and so do you," Charlotte said.

"The boyfriend who forced her to into action, to show both him and herself that she could recover," I said, and Missy nodded.

"That's part of it," Charlotte continued. "The man that I choose must have the courage to let me grow. I will grant him that freedom too, and accept the risk that we will develop in opposite directions.

"I think that marriage works best when both people delight in each other's changes. They don't seek the illusion of security by trying to eliminate differences. A relationship can't be secure by trying to hold onto what was, or in fearing what might be.

"I certainly wouldn't object to a man with great looks or wealth. But I would insist on him having the other characteristics too," Charlotte concluded, with a small smile.

"That sounds awfully wise," Missy said.

"Well, it's good that I gained something in exchange for my wrinkles," Charlotte said, again with a smile.

"You're beautiful and I don't see any wrinkles!" I insisted.

To this comment, Charlotte just smiled again.

Chapter 59

"What will I do if my parents cut me off? I have no money. I'll have to drop out of school, pregnant and without skills," Missy said, tearfully, as soon as we reached our dorm room.

"Charlotte has offered to help and I'll do what I can," I replied.

"I *won't* take money. My mother always said, 'never borrow money or underwear.'"

Despite the seriousness of her predicament, I burst out laughing at her ridiculous statement.

"*Offer* you my underwear? We're not the same size!" I said, with a deadpan expression.

Missy's face immediately changed to a smile and then she laughed. She is tough and will be OK whatever happens, I told myself.

"When do your parents arrive?" I asked.

"This evening, around six. We're going out to dinner."

"Are your brothers coming too?" I asked.

Missy nodded.

I'd been through sticky situations with my parents. The worst was when I informed my dad that Hillary, my friend since childhood, was pregnant. I had told him this early in the morning, in the kitchen when we were alone.

He was stirring a pot of oatmeal and had nearly dropped the spoon before beginning his lawyerly interrogation of me. It took a while for him to learn the facts since I wasn't being helpful. I didn't want to repeat Hillary's claim: that her baby's father was former President Clinton with whom she had long been obsessed.

My dad took this bombshell with the calm of an experienced lawyer who has heard everything. He suggested that we not tell my mother, who tends to be nervous, and I agreed. Then he offered to help Hillary and promised to keep her secret.

But unlike Missy's father, my dad isn't a Mormon bishop. Church members are expected to have model families, not a pregnant teenager.

"It would be best to be alone with your parents when telling them. I'll meet them downstairs and send them to our room. I'll take your brothers on a tour of the campus," I suggested.

Missy nodded agreement and returned to knitting the pink baby sweater that she had begun. She believed that her parents would be easier on her after learning that her child would be a girl. Missy was the only girl in her large extended family.

Well...maybe. Whether her belief was correct or not, a suitable delusion can help a person survive a fear, I thought.

Chapter 60

When dealing with people you can never be sure what will happen. You may think that you know but this is a misbelief unless the situation is ordinary. Like when you ask your mother to pass the ketchup at home. When asking this of a stranger in a restaurant, I wouldn't risk a bet.

So I wasn't sure how Missy's parents would react. When she and they finally came downstairs, I still didn't know. All were unusually quiet.

Missy later told me what happened and it had been as big a surprise for her as it was for me.

Missy had been wearing her usual concealing clothes when they met. Judged by appearance alone, she had undoubtedly seemed the daughter that they had expected to see.

"They asked how I liked the City and how my studies were going and if I had decided on a career. I answered 'yes,' 'great,' and 'no,' before breaking down crying. Answering ordinary questions when I felt that my life was falling apart was driving me crazy. I sat on my bed, they sat on your bed, and I told them right out. 'I'm pregnant and will keep my daughter.'

"In the silence that followed they just stared. It was like they had met a space alien and had no idea how to communicate with them. Their *virginal, upstanding* daughter being pregnant? No, it wasn't possible!

"There wasn't the yelling and screaming that I had expected and felt that I deserved. Instead, my mother became tearful and hugged me. My father said that it had been their fault that I hadn't trusted them enough to tell them. 'We'll help you in any way we can,' he said."

"Do you like Aunt Avalee and her oldest son, Brock?" my mother asked.

"Yes, and he's a darling. Has he gotten his Ph.D. yet?"

"He will, in June. Avalee was sixteen when she gave birth. He's a wonderful boy and she blesses the day that he was born. When Avalee married four years later, her husband adopted him and treats him no differently than he does their own children. Brock has never known his real father," my mother said.

"I just stared, having had no idea. I had always sensed that Aunt Avalee looked too young to have a son that age but had simply assumed that she had good genes," Missy told me.

Missy's dad had asked about the father of her baby and she told him the truth. That her despair about Odis' disappearance had led her into the arms of her school counselor who has now disappeared.

At this revelation, her father simply nodded. He asked about her health and whether she had a doctor and she assured him about both.

"I told them that I planned to continue at Barnard after the baby was born, and of Charlotte's offer. When they learned that she was Mormon, the tension in the room seemed to evaporate.

"Then my dad said, 'Come. We have to feed you and your daughter and tell your brothers that they'll soon be uncles.' Then I began crying and my mom cried and we all hugged.

"My dad said that while we can't control everything that happens to us we can control how we respond. He said that as we are tried and tested, our character becomes more Godlike, and that he had absolute faith in me."

When the three of them came downstairs, their faces were peaceful, as if they had undergone a religious experience. Her father took us to a Buddhist vegetarian restaurant, Kajitsu, on 9th Street in the East Village. Its hushed interior of earthy beige walls and stone floor added to the evening's spiritual feeling.

Yes, miracles still happen, I told myself.

Chapter 61

After leaving the restaurant, we passed an old building that was surrounded by men. Though their ages varied from young to elderly, their clothing was identical and of 19th century style: black cloth jacket, black trousers, white shirt, and tall, black fur hat.

Missy's father explained what was happening.

"It's a Hasidic funeral. They're a sect of Judaism. In the Jewish religion, cremation is forbidden and burial takes place as soon as possible after death. The body isn't displayed before burial and flowers aren't brought.

"In Israel, the service begins at the burial grounds but elsewhere it can originate at a funeral home or a cemetery or a synagogue or a yeshiva. That's a Jewish school. The procession accompanies the body to the place of burial. This is referred to as *levayah* which means *escorting*. It suggests that there is commonality among the souls of the living and the dead."

We silently watched, our heads bowed in prayer.

Death seemed to envelop us even after we passed the synagogue.

"Forty years ago, right here, there was a notorious murder of a young college couple. The area has been redeveloped since," Missy's father remarked, with the authority of his guide book expertise.

I suggested walking to 14th Street before getting a taxi. It was a short distance and no one objected.

We sauntered along the street, I accompanying her brothers while Missy walked behind with her parents. I was entranced by the individuality of the shops and passersby until hearing a sharp "no" from Missy. I turned toward her. She stood frozen, looking shattered, as her mother held her.

Only after the taxi had dropped her parents and brothers off at their hotel did I learn what upset her.

"My father has scheduled Odis' memorial service tomorrow at Manhattan's Mormon Church. But I *know* he's alive. Sending me a charm every birthday is his way of saying that we'll be together again."

I nodded and said nothing for there was nothing that I could say. Randy believed that Odis was alive and that was good enough for me. Sooner or later we would know for sure.

"I'll come with you to the ceremony," I said.

"I'll invite Constance and Artur. Now, they're my family too," Missy said.

Again, I simply nodded.

Chapter 62

By tradition, Mormons don't have memorial services but one had been scheduled for Odis on the following day. After the Sunday morning worship and group meetings, we met in a small room that was little different from a classroom except for the gorgeous view of Central Park from its windows. There, those who had known Odis joined together to bear witness to his life. Not to parade his academic achievements but to state what he had meant to them.

Odis' father spoke first, for both parents. His speech was followed by moving talks from each of his brothers. They revealed how much he had advanced their lives and the loss they felt.

When the last of the brothers had spoken, the ward's (congregation's) bishop rose to close the ceremony with a few words. But before he had reached the lectern, Missy unexpectedly rose and said that she would like to speak. This hadn't been scheduled because of her upset the previous evening. Missy's mother looked toward her husband and he shrugged.

The ceremony had been conceived to comfort Missy. To end her continuing, troubling belief that Odis remained alive and to foster closure. I began doubting that this was to be.

"Odis was more than an older brother to me," Missy said, in a clear, strong voice. "He was my teacher and confidant. He had courage, a 'can do' attitude, and a resolve to succeed, timeless values that he tried to instill in me.

"He was modest to others but was my hero. I loved him for what he demonstrated: the determination to succeed against odds, fair play, the desire to serve our community and nation, and the ability to love deeply. Despite his long absence, *I am convinced that he lives!*"

Then, with unbent back and head held high, Missy left the lectern and walked from the room. She looked at no one.

Chapter 63

Nobody said anything after Missy left the room. All filed out quietly. When I went looking, I found her in the church's anteroom. She was drying her eyes.

"I'm OK. I get tearful when speaking about Odis," she said, trying to force a smile to her face.

I nodded, and touched her hand.

"Will you be going to lunch with us?" I asked.

"Absolutely! I love Indian food and Cordelia does too," she said, touching her stomach.

Because choosing a restaurant can be hard if only one person in a family is vegetarian, these families usually choose Indian or Chinese cuisine. There, it is possible to find something to please everyone. Missy's parents learned this lesson years before. The restaurant that they chose had more than fifteen vegetarian specials. This is about fourteen more vegetarian dishes than at restaurants serving American food.

Dawat was within walking distance, on East 58th Street. Its awning advertised its specialty as "Haute Cuisine Of India."

Three tables were moved together to accommodate our group. Missy's father made the only comment about what happened earlier.

"Funerals and memorials are intended to comfort the survivors and help them move on with their lives. The deceased live always, in our memories," he said.

Being a bishop, Missy's father could have spoken of the Mormon belief in an afterlife but he didn't. That wasn't his role that day.

For starter, I ordered Aloo Tikkyas, which is potato cakes with red pepper chutney and almonds and mint. Missy had Vegetable Samosa which consists of spicy seasoned potatoes and peas wrapped in pastry. On the table were plates of Paneer Kulcha (tandoori bread stuffed with seasoned cheese) and Vegetable 'Harra Bhara' Kebab (green vegetables, potatoes, and Indian cottage cheese patties spiced with pear chutney). I tried not to fill up on these.

Both Missy and I chose the vegetarian lunch special while the others chose lamb, chicken, and fish dishes. We drank water and Lassi (a cold yogurt drink). For dessert I had Gulab Jamun (a pastry made with honey) and the others had Kheer (rice pudding with pistachios and flavored with cardamom) or Kufi (Indian ice cream).

We stood outside the restaurant after our splendid meal. We didn't want to separate but also not to tire Missy.

"Greenacre Park on East 51st Street. We can sit there," I suggested, and that's where we went.

Chapter 64

Greenacre Park is one of Manhattan's gems. Though small, just sixty feet by one-hundred-twenty feet, it has a twenty-five foot waterfall and running stream, seating, an elegant stone sculpture wall, and a food vendor. What more could you want?

We sat on the raised level. The City's noise was hushed by the falling water. Conversation began with Missy's question.

"Have you read *Spinster*?" she asked Charlotte.

"You consider me *a spinster*?" Charlotte replied, with a smile.

"Only in the best sense of the word," Missy said, returning her smile.

Tristan looked up from the game that he was playing on his IPhone. He had sensed something in his mother's tone.

"Yes, I read the book and it doesn't describe me," Charlotte said. "Many of the women that the author refers to have had unstable lives and marriages. One lived on the streets and never had a home of her own. She had lived in boarding houses or with random other women in dorm-like settings. Do I seem like that?"

"Just the opposite!" I insisted, perhaps more loudly than I should have. Charlotte didn't need me to defend her.

"Instead of describing the experiences of the ninety-nine percent of single women who were never married or not-yet-married or are divorced, the author tells us about her life: her boyfriends, depression, and being helped by her wealthy father. She moved back home when she was in her thirties.

"That isn't my life, and it's not the life of most singles who don't dine at trendy restaurants and party their evenings away. My exhausting nights are filled with medical emergencies. I don't even have time for the online dating that the author never needed though she's older than me."

Tristan's eyes had turned back to his video game. It would be years before this adult topic interested him.

"Don't you feel the need for a husband to share your life with?" Missy's mother asked.

"*Absolutely*, and I once thought that I had it but our relationship washed up. It couldn't handle the changes in society that were occurring," Charlotte replied.

"How so?" Missy's father asked, with noticeable interest. Counseling couples is an important duty of a Mormon bishop.

"He was a lawyer and a very good one. While he was in law school and I was in medical school, we supported each other by taking turns with chores. But after his graduation, I was expected to support his career by being the equivalent of a stay-at-home wife who took his clothes to the cleaners and baked cookies. I couldn't be what he wanted and he ignored my career.

"Marrying him would have been a disaster for both of us. He would have viewed me as an inadequate wife and I would have been this for him. The problem might have been that we didn't respect ourselves enough. Maybe if we had, we would have needed less from each other. We were like ships passing in the night," Charlotte concluded, with a hint of regret.

Randy had been sitting beside me, listening attentively. When Charlotte stopped speaking and the others had turned toward a loudly arguing couple on the floor below, he leaned closer and whispered in my ear.

"I decrypted more of Odis' diary yesterday. I now know why he disappeared," he said.

Chapter 65

Randy's whisper told me that he wanted us to be alone when we spoke. That he was unsure how Missy would react to the facts he had discovered. No one wanted a repetition of her meltdown that day.

The hours passed slowly, like when one awaits the results of a critical medical test. We were finally alone, seated in our dorm's lounge with sound from the sixty-inch TV to overwhelm eavesdropping.

"What?" I asked Randy, expectedly.

"I have bad and good news," he said, taking my hand. "Much of what I read concerns his girlfriend: she wanting them to become engaged, how many children she wants, where they could live, her hopes for their future."

"Which never happened," I said, interrupting him, hoping that their fate would not be ours.

"No, their future never happened," Randy said somberly. "The good news is that I'm now more than ever convinced that Odis is alive. He had pieced out the sole source of multiple crimes—murders, kidnappings, robberies, drug and child trafficking—but reached a dead end. The criminals learned that he was studying them and they began searching for him.

"He felt the only way that he could gain safety for himself and his family was by gaining evidence of their crimes and informing the authorities. 'I will travel to the devil's womb,' he wrote. That was his final sentence. He has a poetic streak."

"OK I understand, but where did he go? Where is he?" I asked, with a tinge of irritation. As I've said, Randy likes to stretch his explanations out.

"*That* I don't know because he didn't say. He only wrote that he was leaving. He was afraid, but excited and confident too. He believed that what he was doing would either change or end his life. He's quite a guy."

"Yes, he is," I agreed.

"I didn't know if you wanted me to tell Missy, considering how emotional she is," Randy said, with a hesitancy that mirrored mine.

"Let me think about it. I don't see this new information as changing anything since she's already convinced that Odis is alive. She doesn't care what he's doing, only with finding him."

"I never want to place you in that position," Randy said.

"If you do, I'll be the one that murders you," I replied.

We didn't talk more. Randy held me until the 11PM news ended. Then he left.

Chapter 66

After returning to my room, I told Missy what Randy learned. The news didn't upset her.

"That doesn't tell us where Odis is, does it?" Missy asked.

I agreed that it didn't, Missy calmly went to bed, and I followed.

A common saying is that things will look better in the morning and this is often true. When you're tired, crazy fears can crop up and problems magnify. So I usually discount nightmares as telling me anything except that I'm dealing with too many problems and am rightly nervous.

Or I might be scared because of something that I'm about to do for the first time or what I sense is about to happen. Maybe a medical condition is worsening, a huge personal battle is beginning, or a human monster has invaded my life or that of someone I love.

Vladimir once told me that if you must battle, it's important to choose the time and the place. "But one doesn't always have this opportunity," he added, solemnly.

Though I couldn't have known, these three shocks were rapidly approaching. One led into the other and the victims were unable to choose the time or place of battle.

The first crisis began when Missy stood up to comment during our English class. Almost instantly she froze, said "dizzy," and wavered. I quickly grabbed her, kicked away the surrounding chairs and lowered her gently onto the ground.

Everyone in the room became immobilized until, for some crazy reason, a girl sought help by pulling the fire alarm beside the door. Then things exploded. People streamed into the corridors until our teacher's message reached the administration: that a student had fainted and the alarm was accidentally pulled.

The police emergency number, 911, was called. Missy soon opened her eyes. She said that she was feeling fine and wanted to get up but I and the teacher (Dr. Chu), who had remained in the room, encouraged her to lay still until the Emergency Medical Services arrived.

While lain on the ground, Missy's attempt to conceal her pregnancy had failed as her loose top rose.

"You're pregnant?" Dr. Chu asked, though the answer was obvious.

Missy nodded.

"How far along are you?"

"Five months."

"Do you have a doctor?"

"Yes."

"Do you live nearby?"

"In the Brooks Hall dorm," Missy replied.

This was Dr. Chu's final question. Looks of sympathy and anxiety passed over her face and I knew what she was thinking. That, though all girls have wombs and sex was known to be rampant in the dorms, pregnancy was forbidden by Barnard edict.

Missy had committed the unpardonable. She had broken a college regulation and Barnard's unforgiving, rule-loving administration would be determined to settle the score.

Chapter 67

The EMS arrived quickly and did their thing. Missy wanted to walk to the ambulance but they insisted on wheeling her there on a stretcher. This created Barnard's scene of the week. Missy insisted that I accompany her in the ambulance and the driver agreed.

The doctor at St. Luke's was warm and seemed capable but his first question astonished us.

"Do you know that you're pregnant?" he asked.

Missy stared at him for several moments before nodding.

"I'm in my fifth month," she said, coldly.

"I'm sorry if my question sounded rude but some girls don't know though we've never had a pregnant Barnard student before. I'll explain what happened.

"During pregnancy, fluctuations of blood pressure can cause dizziness or fainting. The hormone, progesterone, dilates veins and your blood pressure drops. This is more likely to happen if you stand quickly.

"The pregnant body has more blood and fluid to accompany the developing baby. This can increase blood pressure, causing headaches or dizziness, and there are other possible causes. As pregnancy advances, the weight of the baby squeezes blood vessels in your legs, pelvis, and body when you lie on your back, making you feel dizzy as your blood pressure drops.

"Being too hot adds to these problems. Overheating is common because the growing baby pushes your normal body temperature up one degree. Does diabetes run in your family?"

"No," Missy replied.

"Good. Occasional fainting or dizziness can be caused by diabetes that one had before becoming pregnant, and gestational diabetes can occur during pregnancy. It's crucial to maintain a stable blood sugar level if one has diabetes.

"Only rarely does fainting or dizziness suggest more serious problems such as an ectopic pregnancy or bleeding from the placenta."

"How can I avoid getting dizzy?" Missy asked.

"Eat regularly, but little and often. Crackers or nuts or a banana are always a safe bet. Avoid sweet, sugary foods. They'll give you a quick fix but lead to a slump in your blood sugar. And drink plenty of water rather than caffeinated drinks such as tea or coffee or cola."

"That's no problem. I'm Mormon and we don't drink those. Is my being vegetarian a worry," Missy asked.

"No, but choose iron-rich foods such as beans and kale to ensure that you don't become anemic, and consider drinking a liquid iron supplement which your body can easily absorb. But speak to your doctor about this first.

"Also, wear layers of loose, comfortable clothing so you can take a layer off if you get too hot. If it's a hot day, drink plenty of water and sponge your face and hands with cool water. Make sure that your bath water isn't too hot and get out of the bath carefully in case you feel dizzy. Never use a spa bath or hot tub. These aren't safe during pregnancy.

"Keep moving to get your circulation going and don't stand for long periods. When sitting, don't cross your legs since this increases your risk of developing a blood clot in your leg."

"Don't sleep flat on your back for long periods since the weight of your womb can press on the large blood vessels returning blood to your heart and restrict your circulation. It also temporarily reduces your baby's oxygen supply."

"What should I do if I do feel faint?" Missy asked.

"Sit with your head between your knees or lay down. Take deep breaths, loosen any tight clothing, and ask someone to place a wet cloth on your forehead. Enough said."

The doctor rose to leave.

"Being an expectant mother is such hard work," Missy drawled slowly, in her soft Southern accent that entrances men.

"Where are you from?" the doctor asked, as if he were now seeing her for the first time as being more than a pregnant body.

"*Charleston*," Missy replied, with a smile, stretching out the syllables and doing all but bat her eyes.

I'm considered pretty but Missy's beauty arouses stares and has caused accidents. Though Artur is her man, habit had made Missy's seductiveness routine when she met an attractive man.

"Honey, you ain't whistling Dixie," the doctor said, with a big grin, before walking off.

Chapter 68

A dozen roses arrived at our room on Saturday.

"Artur plans to bring me roses on the monthly anniversary of the day we met. It's the wrong day but it's the spirit that counts," Missy explained, when I questioned the flowers.

Pregnant women are a unique species and related to differently. Many people stare, some feel that pregnant bellies are a communal resource and can be touched, and others freely ask questions that they would never ask of another stranger.

All three reactions occurred on campus. And, just as had happened to my English father when he became famous, Missy discovered that she had friends that she had never known. Missy, simply by nature of her expanding belly, had become cherished–though not by all.

Not all people agree on everything. As I had learned in my high school History class, two-thirds of Americans were either neutral or opposed the American Revolution. Similarly, there was a split in attitude on the Columbia-Barnard campus. Here, Missy's appearance would produce smiles and offers of help but also avoidance.

Some feared to socialize with a pregnant student. They knew of the college's ban on pregnant undergraduates and feared the administration's reaction.

School was their life and to attend elite Barnard College was a girl's equivalent of attending Harvard or Yale where many of their boyfriends studied. What would happen to Missy? What might happen to them if they became too friendly with her?

At first nothing did happen except that Missy became an object of curiosity. Our dorm room became the favored hang-out of First-Year girls asking variations of the same question: What does it feel like to be pregnant?

Having unknown students spontaneously drop into our room became so distracting that Missy scheduled an informal Q&A about pregnancy in the Lounge. The overflow crowd led to a request for an interview from the *Columbia Daily Spectator*.

Knowing of my interest in becoming a writer, Missy insisted that I interview her. The resulting article, *What Every Woman Should Expect Upon Becoming Pregnant,* was published and achieved wide circulation online.

"Let's begin with psychology. What are your strongest feelings while pregnant?" I asked Missy, this being the first question of our interview.

Despite her demure upbringing, my questions caused Missy to burst out about her experience.

"I feel terrified and excited at the same time. I feel a closeness with penguins since we both waddle, and with Jabba the Hutt since we look the same. I have dreams in which I'm friendly with space aliens, and get used to sleeping in a fortress of pillows.

"I feel awe at my ability to create a human being and feel life growing inside me. But I also can't wait for my pregnancy to be over even if the worst pain of my life is coming,

"I tend to cry when little things goes wrong and feel like punching strangers who comment on my body. Is that enough?" Missy had asked me.

"You're doing fine! Now, what are your new bodily sensations?" I asked.

I had adopted the role of TV interviewer though she was lying on the bed while I sat in a beanbag.

Missy thought for a moment.

"Well, I've learned that morning sickness can last, that pantiliners aren't just for periods, and that a woman can get diaper rash even when she's not wearing diapers. I always feel hot. I have to pee about every fifteen minutes, and pee a little when I cough or sneeze. I seem to plan every trip with the location of clean bathrooms. I've been told that getting diarrhea means that the baby might be coming soon and am afraid of this since I'm still early."

Despite being a virgin, I nodded with understanding. I had more than enough information for my article but wanted a final comment to sum up. "What is the most important thing that you learned from being pregnant?" I asked.

Missy thought for several moments before answering.

"I've learned that it is possible to love someone deeply even before you meet them," she replied.

I could hardly wait until my article was published and I became recognized as a writer. Missy could hardly wait until her pregnancy was over. The administration could hardly wait until Missy left Barnard, and their action came first.

Chapter 69

The envelope was addressed to Missy. It had been hand-delivered by our dormitory's First-Year Focus Director. The enclosed letter stated that, by being pregnant and living in a campus dormitory, Missy had violated Rules 14A, B, and C of Barnard's disciplinary code, the penalty for which could be expulsion. If she chose to leave the college voluntarily, this violation would be removed from her record, thus easing her transfer to another college.

Her affirmative answer was required within one week. If she refused to leave, she would be notified of the date for her hearing before Barnard's Disciplinary Committee. It was obvious what their decision would be.

"I *won't* leave. I tried so hard to be admitted. I was first in my high school class during the last three years," was Missy's tearful reaction.

I hesitated before speaking, being ignorant of what a college could or could not do. But I *was* certain of one thing.

"You need a good lawyer," I told her.

"I don't know a lawyer and even if I did I couldn't afford them," she wailed.

"Trust me. I know a very good lawyer," I said assuredly, for I did.

My father is considered an excellent lawyer. Years before, he had kept Randy from being expelled from high school–and possibly jailed–because of a favor he did for a deceitful friend.

I phoned my dad and, after the usual family chit-chat, explained why I had called.

"If Missy doesn't leave Barnard voluntarily, the college intends to expel her for being pregnant," I said, breathlessly.

"They can't do that," my dad said, calmly.

"Well, they're certainly trying and she needs a great lawyer and you're licensed to practice in New York. Will you help her? *Please.*"

I drawled out the syllables of "please," having learned as a child that this tends to work with my father.

"Alright. Come visit and I'll speak with her," my dad replied.

"She can't afford to pay," I cautioned, wanting to be upfront about this.

"There'll be no charge for I'll owe her. Upon graduating from law school, lawyers view themselves as being guardians of justice but become cynical over the years. Helping Missy will remind me of why I became a lawyer."

I was silent for a few moments, feeling too moved to speak. Finally, I spoke softly.

"We'll be up on Saturday. I love you dad, I really do," I said.

"And I'll always love you no matter how many scrapes you get into," my dad replied.

"*Oh, dad,*" I said, before hanging up and turning toward Missy.

"My father will handle your case. We'll see him in Greenwich on Saturday. Now calm down and let's eat. Cordelia must be hungry," I said.

Chapter 70

Artur offered to rent a car and drive us to Greenwich but Missy wouldn't let him.

"You have two exams on Monday and they must be your priority," she had told him, already acting as the wife that they both expected her to become.

But his offer wasn't needed since traveling to Greenwich from Manhattan is no problem. Trains leave regularly from Grand Central Station and the ride is less than an hour. My backpack was filled with Missy's bottles of water and snacks as we left the dorm at a little after 8AM. We took the 7th Avenue subway line to 42nd Street, then transferred to the Cross-Town Shuttle. It took us across 42nd Street to Grand Central Station.

After our experience with the subway thugs, we became nervous riding it but nothing unpleasant happened. Missy's pregnancy had made her even more beautiful and a young man who offered her his seat tried to chat her up. He had obviously hoped to get her phone number until realizing that she was pregnant.

"Motherhood turns men off. I may not have a sex once Cordelia is born," Missy remarked, after the man left the train.

I had no answer. My Internet based sex knowledge goes only so far.

The trains to Greenwich leave from the lower level of Grand Central Station. That floor contains mostly food stalls but some stores too and I bought the local Greenwich newspaper.

Missy napped and I read during the ride. The newspaper didn't report any train problems or power outages and good weather was predicted.

I had convinced Missy to spend the weekend with my family. I wanted to remove her from the circus that her presence aroused on campus. I searched the paper for events that would take Missy's mind off her worries.

Greenwich High School was staging *Grease* and seeing that was an inexpensive possibility. Bruce Museum was having an Outdoor Crafts Festival but Missy wasn't a crafts person and wouldn't feel comfortable walking for hours. The other events were, as is usual for Greenwich, too expensive for us to attend. Like they say about buying a yacht: if you must ask the price, you can't afford it.

I was looking forward to spending the weekend with my family. Say what you will about families, for me and almost everyone else they are home.

I awakened Missy as the train approached the Greenwich station. She woke with a start and a look of fright.

"We're here," I said, reassuringly.

"I had a nightmare," she said, as her eyes began to focus.

"Everyone has nightmares when they're going through a lot," I said.

"That I am," Missy replied, as the train ground to a halt.

Despite Missy's protest, I carried our luggage. I didn't want her carrying anything. Cordelia was growing steadily.

Chapter 71

My mother picked us up at the station. I pointed out the sights as we drove up the main street, Greenwich Avenue.

"It's beautiful, very green like Charleston," Missy said, and I felt pleased.

"It's a wonderful town. You'll love it," I said.

"You might consider settling here someday," my mother added.

One of my mother's major interests is increasing the town's tiny Mormon population.

But we had come to Greenwich on business and my father took charge soon after greeting us. He and Missy held their legal discussion in his home office from which I was barred. I knew that an attorney must speak alone with their client to maintain confidentiality. If anyone else sits in on their meeting, this privilege is lost.

While waiting, I became part of my family again. My sisters described events in their lives while we munched my mother's peanut butter cookies.

Missy re-joined us an hour later, looking happier than when she arrived.

"Your dad had me tell my story. Then he described the Individuals with Disabilities Education Improvement Act of 2004 which requires that a fair, objective hearing be held. He said that while he rarely tells a client this and can't guarantee it, he believes that I have nothing to worry about."

I learned more that night during dinner when my dad spoke of what Missy confronted.

"Like other large organizations, many schools view themselves as being a world apart. They think that they can treat students as they please without interference but this isn't true," my dad insisted.

"Isn't it? There was a story in today's paper about a teacher who was fired from a Catholic school after marrying her girlfriend," I countered, knowing that my father loves a good argument.

"Ah, but that was a religious school and they claimed an exemption for their behavior, stating that their teachers' behavior must reflect the wisdoms of their religion. They had classified their teachers as having a religious role. This made it a gray areas legally."

I knew when to give up and raised my hands in mock surrender.

My oldest sister, Melody, who attends New York University's Film School, took up the battle.

"Wouldn't a student's case fall under contract law? They pay tuition in exchange for an education. If this is interrupted unfairly, wouldn't the student have cause to sue the college for damages? I read on the Internet about two girls who are suing their college's sonogram program for harassment. They refused to sample invasive vaginal exams during a required course and had to drop out of school.

"Missy could also sue for the stress that the school's behavior has created and is affecting her fetus' development."

I was stunned by her arguments. My father grinned broadly.

"Melody, you *must* consider a legal career," my dad said. "*Do* graduate from film school but then attend law school and practice entertainment law. You'll be dealing with movie big shots and can teach film in your spare time. That's what many multi-talented people do.

"Wallace Stevens, the great poet, worked as an insurance executive all his life. He refused an appointment at Harvard which would have enabled him to write full-time. He preferred writing, his labor of love, to be a hobby."

"That's a *great* idea," Melody said enthusiastically, and my dad looked pleased.

One less child to have to worry about, he might have been thinking. After several moments of silence, I put in my two cents

"I'd solve Missy's problem in a different manner and more quickly than by suing or threatening it," I said.

I waited until gaining everyone's attention before continuing.

"I'd go to war!"

Chapter 72

My father smiled at my comment. My daughters are certainly poles apart, he was probably thinking.

I began my argument.

"Missy needs Barnard to end their nonsense *now*. Getting them to do this legally takes time and adds to her stress. Even if she wins in the end, what will be the effect on her baby?

"We must pressure the school to do what's right. It's likely that many officials don't even know what's happening and would be her side. We don't know who began this affair but know how it must end. Our campaign will help Barnard recognize this.

"'Barnard Bans Babies' could be our motto though I'm open to others. We'll make a YouTube video with a cute child asking her older, pregnant sister why Barnard hates babies and whether they hate her too. We'll have buttons reading, 'Barnard hates babies. Do you?'

"Hopefully, the school will back down quickly, maybe using the excuse that their letter was poorly worded. Say that they *never* wanted Missy to leave Barnard."

There was silence as my suggestion was considered. The first person to speak was my gorgeous eight-year-old sister, Claudine. "Does Barnard hate me too?" she asked, in a sad tone, her eyes wide open.

Melody entered the drama, "No, darling, only *some* people who work there do," she said, in an equally sad voice, her hands clasped over her belly.

"We'll make the video today!" Melody exclaimed, as my dad grinned.

And that's what happened.

"The Sony CX900 camcorder that the film school lent me will be perfect for this. It's has a back-illuminated 1.0 type sensor, a 50 Mbps XAVC S format, a 29mm wide angle Zeiss Vario-Sonnar lens, a BIONZ X image processing engine, Dolby surround sound, a lens ring for smooth zooming, and manual controls. It also has Wi-Fi/NFC for easy sharing," Melody explained, though none of us understood.

"But we'll need a script," she added.

"I'll write it," I volunteered.

Our battle began. Melody couldn't operate the camera since she would be playing a starring role so my other sister, fourteen-year-old Melanie, was asked to do this. She agreed, and suggested that a graphic rape scene be added to increase the likelihood of our video going viral. Missy's frown, my mother's glare, and my father's head shake damned this eye-catching idea.

Over the next hour, Melody taught Melanie how to use the camcorder, Claudine decided on the clothes that she would wear, and I wrote the script. For the few of you who haven't seen the video, it goes like this.

First comes a close-up of Claudine's angelic face, then the image of Melody's pregnancy-shaped belly. This was accomplished with a small pillow.

To Melanie's delight, her suggestion that our star be bra-less and wear a tight blouse *was* followed. This enabled a good cleavage shot to gain the male audience. Melody has her arm about Claudine's shoulder as the child looks up and asks, "Why does Barnard hate babies?" "Not everyone there does," Melody replies. "If I go to Barnard, does that mean that my baby cousins can *never* visit me there?" Claudine asks. "Pray, that someday they may," Melody replies.

Fade to black.

Chapter 73

Despite the overlain tension created by Missy's problem, the weekend was wonderful. Randy came down from Yale, Erika came over with her boyfriend, Clarence, and Hillary brought her baby, Angelica, who was thriving. She was born prematurely and her survival had been chancy, to say the least.

In the basement rec room where we had hung out in the past, Hillary and Missy bonded about pregnancy and Randy sought Clarence's help with decrypting Odis' files. Randy is a gifted hacker but readily admits that Clarence is a class unto himself.

The day's enthusiasm extended to Melody who couldn't wait to show her video production. We viewed it after my brief explanation of Missy's problem ("Missy is pregnant and lives in a dorm. Barnard wants to expel her for violating college rules.")

Melody transferred the video from the camcorder to her laptop and pressed the play button. Silence filled the room when the video ended. No cheers or applause, not even boos. Finally, Erika spoke.

"It's *brilliant*. My dad taught math at Columbia before moving to Wall Street. He'll call people on your behalf."

Erika's father is Greenwich's resident billionaire. Missy can hardly do better than having him as an ally, I thought.

"Thank you," Missy said, softly, and tears filled her eyes as cheers erupted.

What began as a family visit turned into a typical school sleepover. Hillary couldn't stay because of Angelica but the others did. To repay my religious mother for the extra work that their presence created, all allowed themselves to be roped into attending service at our local Mormon church the following day.

This *was* a courtesy since Randy, Clarence, and Erika rarely attend church. Christmas service for their families consists of brunch at a restaurant with a top Zabar rating.

We separated after church. Erika's father had scheduled brunch for her and his new girlfriend, and Randy had to return to school. My parents dropped Missy and me off at the railroad station and we caught the next train to Manhattan.

"Your dad said that he'd fax a letter to Barnard's president tomorrow. When do you think we should upload the video onto YouTube?" Missy asked.

"In a few days. I'm ordering buttons and banners online and we can't work from the dorm. The college might say that we're running a business and try to throw us both out. But our supplies shouldn't cost much. I mean, how many can we need?"

Plenty, as it turned out.

Missy phoned Artur from the train and mentioned our need for office space. He suggested using a room in his parents' Manhattan apartment but said that he'd have to check with them. So the first stop that we made after arriving at Grand Central Station was their apartment.

Missy described our problem to Artur's parents and what we needed. They readily agreed after viewing the video that I had brought from Greenwich on a USB drive.

"We're going to war," I said, having become taken with this phrase.

"Russians are used to war, and you have a good story. I could tell it to a journalist friend and give him a copy of your video. That would be the way to go if you want publicity," Ivan said.

Thus Barnard's attack on Missy first became news not on American TV but on *RT*, the Russian government's television station. It had its own reason for wanting this story. As their "breaking news of the day," a beautiful busty announcer described "America's assault on another of its students."

With that, and our war began.

Chapter 74

We were leaving the apartment when Charlotte phoned. She had been called into work later that evening and asked if I could babysit. I readily agreed and took an Uber taxi to her home while Missy returned to campus.

The hushed lobby was a welcome relief from the City's clamor, a quiet which extended to Charlotte's apartment. She was reading a medical journal and Tristan was busy building another Raspberry Pi project when I arrived.

I shared Missy's college problem with Charlotte, hoping to recruit her as an ally. The support of a Columbia University Medical School obstetrician would benefit our cause.

Tristan entered the room while I was setting up the video for viewing. I instantly had another brainstorm. Tristan would star in a new version of the video. He would hold Claudine's hand in the final scene. She would look into his eyes and say, "Someday, grownups will believe in love too."

"*Yes,*" I screamed aloud, to their astonishment. I had the reputation of being well-behaved, not a crazed artist.

"I'm sorry. I just had an idea for another scene. But it would involve Tristan and be up to the two of you," I explained.

Through my babysitting experiences I've learned that every mother considers their child beautiful and loves to show them off. Though a doctor, Charlotte was no different. Tristan's cooperation was gained with a bribe: he could play with the camcorder. I phoned Melody and arranged for her to bring Claudine into Manhattan.

The photo shoot took place at Charlotte's apartment and it couldn't have gone better. The children stared lovingly into each other's eyes, and mine were moist when their scene ended. After snacks, Tristan showed Claudine his Raspberry Pi inventions and she listened with adoration.

"You may have made a match," Charlotte whispered to me during dinner.

"Maybe Tristan prefers older girls," I whispered back.

Claudine is a year older than Tristan.

Chapter 75

Our campaign grew like an avalanche, slowly at first but gradually picking up strength. The showing of the first video produced some reaction but not as much as we had hoped. Marketing is a skill that must be learned and my ignorance was total. Even so, apart from a few viewer comments that I won't dignify with repetition, the response was good.

The video was considered professional and the script was praised. Melody was awarded class credit for its production. It was the second video with Tristan that did it. Also, by then I had learned about hashtags.

#helpgirl, *#don'tbanbaby*, *#collegemom*, *#pregnanthelp*, and *#loveforall* gained viewers and our statistics rose. The day after Missy's mention on Russian TV, there were one-hundred-sixty-one views of the video and nineteen E-mails. By the second day, this figure had nearly doubled and on the third day, after I uploaded the second video, the numbers exploded.

Hits were in the five figure range that day, the six figure range two days later, and by the weekend it had gone viral, gaining millions of views around the world.

"You'll rival Taylor Swift if it keeps going like this," Randy told me.

He had been monitoring the statistics and locations of viewers. It wasn't a surprise that most of them were in the United States since the video was in

English. What did surprise us were the many viewers in Dubai and Calcutta and Johannesburg and points in between.

"English has become a worldwide language," my high school English teacher had said, and our experience evidenced this.

Being reluctant to further inflame the Barnard authorities by giving out buttons and banners on campus, Missy and I handed them out from two popular Fifth Avenue locations. One was in front of the Metropolitan Museum of Art and the second was at the fountain before the Plaza Hotel.

Melody brought Claudine into town on weekends and they and Tristan joined us. Each child held one end of a banner reading, "Help Missy *Now*," while the adults handed out supplies.

While people like getting something for free, I prefer thinking that those who took our buttons and banners believed in our cause.

We soon ran out of supplies and had no money to buy more. But, as they say, miracles *can* happen. Upon returning to our dorm, Missy found a letter containing a check for ten-thousand dollars from the Odysseus Foundation.

It was an organization that neither of us had ever heard of. We knew that Odysseus was the legendary Greek king of Ithaca and a hero of Homer's epic poem, *The Odyssey*. What did that have to do with Missy?

Missy was reluctant to cash the check ("What if it's a scam?") until Randy investigated. By hacking, he discovered that Erika's billionaire father was among the foundation's officers. Mystery solved.

Chapter 76

"It's amazing what we accomplished knowing nothing about promotion," Missy said, when I told her of the huge number of views that our video had achieved.

"Not really, we're a lot older than seven," I replied.

Missy gave me a puzzled look, thinking that I was having one of my brain lapses until I explained.

"A seven-year-old girl, Brooke, caught her friends staring at her food tray in school. They were hungry but didn't have money to buy food and she began buying them food with money in her account. When it faded more quickly than usual, her mother asked what was going on."

"She feared that her daughter was dealing pot," Missy suggested, with a grin.

"Well, maybe. Her mother learned that Brooke was buying food for hungry students and discovered that many kids were given a free lunch. Brooke's parents decided to help.

"They began a foundation that packs a thousand meals a week for schoolkids in the Tampa area. Brook's father owns a car dealership and an empty building on his property serves as headquarters. Area businesses donate money and the foundation gets food at greatly reduced prices. All that began with a seven-year-old's upset at what she saw."

My story of a saintly family aroused just a nod from Missy. She obviously had something personal on her mind.

"I know that since I'm pregnant I shouldn't, but I can't help worrying about Odis," she said.

I just nodded, having nothing reassuring to say. Odis could be alive, as Missy and Randy believed, or he might not. Even if he was alive, we couldn't help him since we didn't know where he was.

But Missy knew this too and her gloom passed quickly.

"Have you heard from my dad or the school?" I asked.

"Nothing. Maybe the video was too nasty and infuriated the administration. Making it might not have been a good idea," Missy said.

"No, it was a wonderful idea!" I insisted. "When battling wickedness, the nastiest person will win."

"Who said that?" Missy asked.

"I did."

Missy stared, and then her face took on the same expression as my mother's upon discovering something unpleasant.

Chapter 77

Three days after our second video went viral, Melody suggested that we needed something new to keep up the pressure on Barnard.

"*People* make decisions, not institutions. Go after their people," she advised us, and we did.

I found the names of Barnard's trustees online and posted these in a postscript to the video. Not to get them harassed but to strengthen the notion that it was real people who were affecting Missy and not nameless bureaucrats.

Moreover, these powerful directors likely didn't watch YouTube and know what was happening. What would they do upon learning that their reputations had been placed at risk?

Melody also proposed a march of concerned students from 110th Street to the Barnard administration building.

"Hold it on a Sunday. It's a slow news day and you'll get more publicity," she said, and that's what we did.

To avoid the need for a parade permit we would ramble on the sidewalk, follow traffic signals, and be quiet. That was my plan.

But as can happen with all campaigns, things went awry. Peaceful protests are prey to attracting troublemakers and we gained our equivalent though no damage was done. In fact, they helped us by attracting far more publicity than we could have hoped.

A contingent of women supporting breast-feeding joined us and nursed their babies along the way. This motivated other women to remove and wave their bras atop their heads as they walked. News photographers were delighted.

Students from Columbia tagged along. They sang a Columbia College song, *Stand Up and Cheer*, when we reached our destination. The reference to "boys" in the song was tactfully changed to "boys and girls."

Two days after our rally, Barnard College gave up. The upset had resulted from unfortunate miscommunication, their attorney's faxed letter to my dad stated. The sole concern of the school had been Missy since a dormitory is not suitable for a baby. Missy is an outstanding student and the idea that she would leave Barnard pained them. How could they help her through this difficult period? Blah, blah, blah...

That night, there was a celebratory party at Community Food & Juice, a highly-rated, organic restaurant on Broadway between 112th and 113th streets. Erika's father had made the arrangements that afternoon and, though his request was last-minute, the restaurant was glad to oblige. Billionaires get this kind of service.

During the party, reporters and photographers granted most of their attention not to Missy but to Claudine and Tristan. Dressed in their finest, they held hands and Claudine made what proved to be the major quote of the event.

"Love and babies have won!" she loudly exclaimed to the high-spirited crowd.

I admit it. I wrote that line.

Chapter 78

Thankfully, the following months were peaceful for a mind can take only so much. Missy no longer attracted attention with her belly now gaining no greater interest than the occasional smile.

Early in her pregnancy, Missy's medical visits had been infrequent. During her first visit to Charlotte's office, a medical history and pap smear were taken.

"Your checkups will be monthly until your sixth month when they'll become weekly. This is more frequent than with most obstetricians but how I prefer to do things. Anytime you have a symptom, that something seems odd, I expect you to call me immediately," Charlotte said, and Missy nodded.

Information was given about the optional prenatal tests and the course of pregnancy. The blood test for sexually transmitted diseases, blood typing, and a urine culture were taken. Thereafter, her weight, blood pressure, urine, and fetal heart tone would be considered at every visit, Missy was told.

"You're healthy and I don't expect you to have any difficulties. I'll sign you up for pre-natal classes. They'll cover signs of pre-term and term labor, breastfeeding, fetal movement counting, pain medication options in labor, and a few more. Do you have any questions?" Charlotte asked.

"Is it OK to have sex during pregnancy?" Missy asked, hesitantly.

"*Absolutely yes*, so long as your pregnancy is proceeding normally. But it may be less frequent since hormonal fluctuations, fatigue, weight gain, nausea, and back pain could sap your desire. Worries about your baby may affect your desire too though a baby is well protected by amniotic fluid in your uterus and its muscles."

"Can having sex cause a miscarriage?" Missy persisted.

"No, early miscarriages are due to chromosomal abnormalities or other problems in the developing fetus," Charlotte replied.

Missy looked embarrassed.

"*What*? Doctors have heard everything," Charlotte asked, with a smile.

"How can we—Artur and I—best have sex while I'm pregnant?" Missy asked.

"The same way that you usually do so long as you're comfortable. Experiment to see what works. Instead of lying on your back, you might lie sideways or atop him.

"The only activities to be cautious about are oral sex and anal sex. If you receive oral sex, make sure that he doesn't blow air into your vagina. Rarely, a burst of air blocks a blood vessel and causes a dangerous condition for the mother and baby.

"Anal sex is best avoided during pregnancy since it could allow infection causing bacteria to spread from the anus to the vagina. It might also be painful if you have pregnancy related hemorrhoids."

Missy didn't mention the worry that she had expressed to me earlier so I did.

"Can orgasms trigger premature labor?" I asked.

"That's a good question, Margaret, and the answer is 'no.' Contractions caused by orgasms are different from those felt during labor. They won't trigger labor even as your due date approaches," Charlotte said, as she rose from her desk.

"Can you make dinner on Saturday? I'd like for you both to be present when I tell Tristan about his father. The issue will seem less charged with the two of you there." Charlotte said.

"I'd love to. I have no plans," I replied.

"I'll be there," Missy agreed.

"About seven," Charlotte said, before leaving the room.

Chapter 79

After Charlotte's invitation, I realized that I was more emotional about Saturday's meeting than I should be since it was *her* event. That night, she would answer Tristan's long unanswered question about his father's identity.

I had been far older than Tristan when I learned the truth about my parents. That my biological father had been an English spy who, it was believed, had been murdered before my birth. That those who I had long believed were my parents had adopted me as an infant, and that my adoptive mother's sister, Aunt Lena, was my biological mother.

These matters had been lain to rest. The truth had outed and I had met and grown to love my biological father and grandmother, as I had always loved my adoptive parents and Aunt Lena.

My present extended family included Vladimir, my courtesy father, and Ulrika, his girlfriend, and Ivan who saved my life in London, and Erika and Randy too. I had learned that, unlike money, the more love you give, the more you have.

"It's a big event for them. I can hardly wait," I said to Missy, as the bus approached.

Missy nodded but didn't answer. She was involved with her own big event.

Tristan was glad to see us on Saturday. While Charlotte put the finishing touches on dinner, he showed us his latest Raspberry Pi project; a wall-mounted Google Calendar.

"It took him days but he finally got it working. We keep his chores on it," Charlotte said proudly.

The dinner was Tristan's favorite: fish cakes with much ketchup and spaghetti, broccoli and spinach, and blueberry yoghurt. When Tristan went to his room to get a new book to show us, Charlotte said, "He'll never be a gourmet but it's better that he's health conscious."

After dinner, Charlotte settled us in the living room for her talk. We waited expectantly, and Tristan seemed to sense that this was not to be an ordinary evening.

"Tristan, you've asked me who your father is and though you'll never meet him, you have the right to know. When I decided to have a child—you—I made sure that your father would be smart and healthy so you would be smart and healthy too—as you are."

"It's not certain," Tristan said, being the genius and devourer of medical texts that he is.

"No, it's not, but my choice made it more likely. I recently hired a lawyer and have gained more information about your father. He has a doctor's degree from Pittsburgh's Carnegie Mellon University," Charlotte said.

"He's a doctor too?" Tristan asked.

"No, not a medical doctor. His degree is in Computer Science and he became a college professor. He is a tall, handsome man, as you will be someday. You have good genes."

"What's his name?" Tristan asked.

"I'll tell you when you're older," Charlotte replied.

Tristan seemed satisfied with this answer. While babysitting, I had learned that when a child asks a question, a brief one or two sentence reply is all they really want.

Charlotte's talk was over.

"Cherry pie?" she asked, and there was no argument.

Chapter 80

"Would that everything went so well. I'll learn more about Tristan's father in a week but was anxious to get our talk over with," Charlotte said.

Missy and I just nodded. This wasn't our ball game.

"I thought that sperm donor information was protected. How did your lawyer get it?" I asked, though sensing how this had been done.

"I didn't ask and said only that I wanted it. His fee was fifty-thousand dollars. Part must have gone to the hacker who entered the company's system," Charlotte said, sheepishly.

Again, I simply nodded. Randy is a gifted hacker and had helped me more than once.

"How are you feeling?" Charlotte asked Missy, abruptly changing the subject.

"Not good. I tend to feel bloated and have an itchy rash on my stomach and sides. It's sometimes so bad that I can't sleep," she replied.

"Bloating is common. Try to rest as much as you can. The rash is called PUPPP, Pruritic Urticarial Papules and Plaques of Pregnancy. It's caused by your elevated progesterone level, and an allergic reaction to your baby's DNA. That's why it disappears after delivery. It can happen during the first pregnancy but almost never with later ones.

"Use a cold, wet towel and corn starch over the area that itches most. If this doesn't help, we can start you on oral steroids. But medications have side effects and it's best to avoid them during pregnancy," Charlotte advised.

We left soon afterward. Charlotte warned that there had been robberies around Central Park. She told us to take an Uber car back to the dorm and we did.

"I wondered why you had a problem sleeping," I said to Missy in the car.

"Yeah, pregnancy is no fun. Thanks for doing my homework," Missy said.

"You have enough worries. You don't need homework too," I said.

Randy phoned just then and I picked up.

"Can you speak now?" he asked, breathlessly.

"Not really, I'm in a cab going back to the dorm," I replied.

"Call me when you get there. Clarence found new information about Odis. He...."

Static crackled on the line and the call abruptly ended.

What a moment for this to happen, I thought. I dreaded hearing what Missy's new worry might be.

Chapter 81

Once in our dorm, Missy got a cold, wet towel for her rash. She wrapped it about her stomach and lay down. I went downstairs to the lounge and phoned Randy from there.

"*What?*" I asked, in a less than friendly tone.

"How is Missy doing?" he asked softly, answering my question with his.

"She's dealing with an itchy rash. What did Clarence find out?"

There was a pause while Randy tried to phrase his words exactly right.

"You know that Clarence is always testing his hacking skills," Randy began.

"Yes, get to it."

"Well, he ran Odis' name through the data base of the New York City Police Department and got a hit. Something...interesting."

"Yes?"

Randy has a hard time getting to the main point of a tetchy conversation.

"Yes. Last night, a duffel bag containing clothing and a wallet were found at a site that's being renovated into apartments."

"OK," I said slowly, already fearing what was coming.

It's useless to try to rush Randy's explanation. If you do, he gets nervous and details are even longer in coming.

"They found Odis' college ID in the wallet," Randy said.

I silently digested what Randy had said. This changed everything. Missy's search for Odis was over. He was dead though we might never learn how or when he died.

"Margaret, are you still there?" Randy asked.

"Yes, I'm thinking. He's dead," I replied.

"Maybe, but there can be no certainty until his body is found. His bag might have been stolen."

"Yes," I reluctantly agreed.

"Will you tell Missy?"

"She has a right to know but I'll wait till morning. Her rash is killing her and she's trying to sleep."

After hanging up, I bought juice from the vending machine and sat. The TV was tuned to the latest City crisis but I wasn't watching. I was thinking of how to tell Missy, and of her likely reaction.

I remembered what Charlotte had told her: "It's crucial to remain calm during pregnancy. Your baby senses your mood and anxious mothers produce nervous children."

Missy and Cordelia will have an agitated morning, I thought.

Missy was sitting up in bed when I returned. She held her phone to her heart.

"My dad just called. The New York City police had phoned him. They said that they found a duffel bag containing Odis' college ID. 'He's surely dead,' my dad said."

I said nothing.

"But we were so close that if he were dead I would *feel* it," Missy pleaded, her eyes brimming with tears.

What she said wasn't logical but I remained silent.

"He's alive, I know he's alive!" Missy screamed.

I remained silent.

After staring into space, Missy hooked her phone into its charger and returned to bed.

Chapter 82

Things remained the same over the following months. I watched over Missy, she watched over Cordelia, and Charlotte watched over Tristan and us. We had become another of those uncommon family units that cities foster. Unrelated people caring for each other as traditional families had done since humanity began.

Artur had become part of our family. He spent increasing time helping Tristan with his Raspberry Pi constructions and joined our Sunday brunch at Charlotte's apartment. These became held every other week at Ivan and Dina's apartment where the cuisine was Russian.

Missy often joined me while I babysat Tristan. Many of her conversations with Charlotte concerned pregnancy.

"It's like having a doctor in the family," Missy remarked to me, and that's what it was.

As winter turned into spring, Missy's rash faded and she looked happier. But I was careful never to mention Odis and felt uneasy about the future. Her birthday, on which she had always received a charm from Odis, was approaching. This gift continued after his disappearance and backed Missy's belief that he lived.

Would Missy receive a charm this year? If she did, what would happen? Would her delusion—as everyone else regarded it—that Odis remained alive be strengthened? If it did not come would Missy collapse into despair?

I waited and worried, thinking that things couldn't get worse. Then they did.

This crisis began late one evening at Charlotte's apartment. Tristan was asleep and I was sitting at the dining room table, studying for a math exam the following day. When Charlotte arrived home, I realized from her face that something awful had happened. Not failing an exam awful but car accident awful.

"What's wrong?" I asked.

Charlotte didn't immediately answer. Instead, she went to the kitchen and returned with a sealed black box and water glass. The expensive, ten-year-old Springbank, 100 proof, single malt Scotch whiskey in the box had been a present from a grateful patient she once told me.

Charlotte seated herself opposite me. She ripped open the box, opened the bottle, and filled her glass a quarter full. She took a sip, made a face, and sipped again. When she turned toward me, her face held such fury that I would not have trusted her to hold a scalpel.

"*The incredible bastard,*" she spat out.

"Who? What happened?" I asked.

It was as if Charlotte were in her own world and hadn't heard me. She sipped more Scotch until her glass was empty.

"I'll see him dead first!" she sputtered, looking directly at me.

I sat silently, awaiting her explanation. When she told me, I could hardly believe it though I did not doubt its certainty.

Chapter 83

The whiskey had its desired effect. Charlotte placed the glass on the table, leaned back in the chair, and closed her eyes.

"I've received more information about Tristan's father–the sperm donor–and it's not good," Charlotte said.

I waited, sensing that more was coming.

"While a graduate student, he donated sperm many times. Tristan has fourteen half-brothers and half-sisters. What the agency promised was true: his father does have a high IQ and was healthy so I can have no claim against them for misrepresentation. It's what he did later...."

Charlotte reached for the whiskey bottle before catching herself and her hand flapped back into her lap.

"You said that he'd earned a doctorate and had an academic career," I objected.

"Yes, that's all true. Until he was fired after being arrested for murder," Charlotte said.

"Murder?" I asked, as if I hadn't heard her correctly.

The word hung in the air.

"The rape and murder of a child. The *one* killing that the police gained evidence of. Four more are suspected."

"OK, so he's in prison. You don't inherit a tendency to murder or rape. Do you have concern about Tristan?" I asked.

"None! He's a wonderful, caring boy. I expect him to have a brilliant future, and give me grandchildren someday. He's not the issue."

There was another silence during which Charlotte swallowed hard.

"The *problem* is that Tristan's father is no longer in prison. He was released two months ago after his new lawyer discovered that the evidence convicting him was tainted by police and prosecutorial misconduct. The search warrant was faulty and evidence that should have been provided to his defense attorney never was.

"Two of the trial's major witnesses now refuse to testify again. The third has disappeared and the police believe that she may have been murdered. There won't be another trial. Tristan's father will remain free."

"OK, but I still don't see how this affects you or Tristan," I said.

"The hacker that my lawyer hired had placed a backdoor–an entrance–into the fertility agency's records. My lawyer had him check Tristan's parentage again. The hacker discovered that the company's system had been recently penetrated. The files selected were those of

Tristan's donor. Someone wanted to identify these children. We don't know why but my lawyer has a good guess."

"What's that?"

"To blackmail these parents. None would want their child's parentage to be publicized in this Internet age. They would be forever damned online as the offspring of a monster," Charlotte said.

Another reason suddenly came to me. One so awful that I hesitated revealing it though knowing that I must.

"I can think of another reason," I said.

Charlotte looked directly at me.

"If there is no new trial, he won't blackmail you to keep Tristan's background secret. He'll want money—a lot of it—to stop him from going into Family Court. He'll seek visitation with Tristan and maybe custody too."

Horror spread over Charlotte's face.

"He'd never get it!" she said, loudly.

"It's a safe bet that he won't get custody since Tristan has always lived with you but there can be no certainty about visitation. That would depend on the judge. But either way his action would shatter your's and Tristan's lives."

Chapter 84

Charlotte wanted to sleep late. She asked me to stay over, to get Tristan off to school in the morning, and I readily agreed.

Charlotte is a good person. She had been helping Missy freely, going far beyond what is expected of a doctor. She had befriended her, and offered her a home. I determined to help Charlotte as best I could.

Moreover, her biggest stress had been caused by my idea that Tristan's father might get visitation with his son. I wasn't sure if this was possible but a lawyer would and my father is a good one.

Lawyers, like doctors, tend to specialize. Though my dad's expertise is maritime law, he's handled other cases. His opinion would be more valuable than mine.

My father goes to sleep early because of his Lyme disease. It was too late to phone him that night and I planned to call him the next morning.

Immediately after walking Tristan to school, I returned to the apartment and phoned my father.

"Do you have a minute or two or three for me?" I asked.

"For you, always. What's up?" he replied.

"Can I run an imaginary legal case past you?" I asked.

I didn't want to place my father in the difficult position of feeling that he should report a crime but not wanting to.

"Shoot," he said, after a momentary pause.

"OK. A woman has artificial insemination and gives birth. Years later, the sperm donor discovers the identity of the woman and seeks custody and visitation of their child. Would a Family Court would grant this?" I asked.

"Well, this really isn't my expertise but I've had some Family Court experience and am up on the law. It would depend on the judge. How old is the child?"

"Seven."

"In that case, since the child has grown up with their mother, it is highly unlikely that any judge would grant the father custody. But he *might* be granted visitation though how much would depend on the judge."

"OK, let me add something to the mix. Let's say that the father was convicted of the rape and murder of a child. He was imprisoned but his conviction was later overturned on technical grounds.

"He's currently free and won't be retried. Past witnesses have refused to testify again. The most important witness has disappeared and is believed to have been murdered. How would a judge rule on visitation now?"

This silence lasted longer.

"That's hard to say. Common sense demands that the request by this parent be dismissed out-of-hand. But that's unlikely since he is the biological father and they have rights regardless.

"There was a New York case twenty years ago in which a jailed murderer sought visitation with his daughter in prison. During the trial, she had been the only witness against him. She saw him murder her mother."

My father paused to let his words sink in. I took a deep breath.

"What happened?" I asked,

"The child's foster care agency went to court and the judge denied the father's request. Common sense occasionally triumphs over law. I would say that in the case you describe, there would be a trial and the mother would win but it's not a sure thing. In the eyes of the law, the father has not been convicted of a crime. What is he like apart from that?" my dad asked, going from the hypothetical to wanting facts.

"Super-wonderful. He has a doctorate in computer science and was a college professor before being fired," I replied.

"The law can be an ass," my father said, sadly.

"Unfortunately," I agreed.

I thanked my father and hung up.

Charlotte didn't awake until after twelve. This might have been from the effect of the whiskey or she not wanting to face the day. I told her my father's opinion when she appeared in the kitchen.

"Some days it doesn't rain, it pours," she said, as she poured a glass of orange juice.

"That it does," I agreed.

Chapter 85

Worries occupied my mind over the following weeks. Some, naturally enough, derived from the approaching exams since keeping my scholarship depended on getting great grades. I forced myself to study but lacked interest.

My thoughts revolved from Missy's pregnancy to Odis' disappearance to Charlotte's possible catastrophe. This, though nothing bad had yet happened. The only good occurrence, and I didn't discount it, was that my family and friends remained healthy and untroubled. Randy had been described as "gifted" by a Nobel laureate professor. This comment made Randy's day and maybe his next decade too.

I told myself not to worry since worrying changes nothing. And, as my dad tells his law clients, "Don't worry until you have to." Missy and Charlotte were capable people. They had survived difficult experiences and I had too.

But I was unable to stop fretting. Part of the reason was my sense that, just as the school term and Missy's pregnancy approached their climax, so did Charlotte's situation. I believed that the stranger who had hacked into the fertility agency's database would soon make their move. All that could be done was to wait.

"We've run out of juice," Missy remarked.

She lay propped up in bed, studying. This was a good sign.

"I'll get it. I need a break," I said, tossing my notebook onto the desk.

There are vending machines in the first floor lounge but I avoid using them whenever possible. It upsets me to pay two dollars for a juice box when you can buy them for so much less at a grocery store a block off campus. Plus, it feels good to get away. Being continually around students is tiring.

While walking slowly to the store, immersed in my thoughts, I received a call from Charlotte. She had been called into work and could I babysit? I agreed, and said that I would be over in a half-hour.

I quickly bought the juice, returned to the dorm, and told Missy. I gathered class notes to study, and a change of clothes if I had to spend the night. The Uber taxi came quickly and I arrived at Charlotte's apartment in a little over a half-hour.

"Have you heard anything?" I asked Charlotte.

Tristan was in the room so we had to speak in code.

"Nothing."

"No news is good news," I said.

"That's the first thing the elderly say when they phone each other, that everything is OK. This waiting is making me old," Charlotte said.

I understood what she felt.

"Battles aren't won through retreat," I said.

"What?"

"A relative of mine said that," I replied.

That was another of Vladimir's bits of advice. Explaining how he came to regard himself as my courtesy father would have taken too much time.

"I don't see any way to attack," Charlotte said, grasping my meaning as she picked up a sleek carryall before leaving.

"I don't either. That's a gorgeous bag."

I couldn't help my comment despite the seriousness of what we had been discussing.

"It's a Grace Bag by Mark Cross. It was inspired by Alfred Hitchcock's masterpiece, *Rear Window*. Have you seen it?"

"Yes. That's one of my sister's favorite movies. The sister who's a film student at NYU."

Rear Window tells the story of a photographer who is temporarily disabled by a broken leg. Feeling bored, he studies the apartments opposite his through binoculars and comes to believe that a murder has been committed. He, his visiting nurse, and his fiancée, Grace Kelly, who later became Princess Grace of Monaco, investigate and... It's a romantic, scary, wonderful movie. Watch it!

I so loved Charlotte's bag that I decided to buy it for Mother's Day. That was my decision until I checked its price online. The bag sold at Barney's for four-thousand dollars. Sorry, mom, that's out of both our financial leagues.

After Charlotte left, I seated myself beside Tristan. He was immersed in his iPad, on his Facebook page that I closely monitored. I put my arm around him. Tristan snuggled and I leaned back and thought.

Chapter 86

At 8:30PM I said that it was time for Tristan to go to bed. He protested but not in the sense that he really objected. He asked that I read him a story. I replied that he had to get ready for bed first and he did. Charlotte has him shower and brush his teeth at bedtime and I made sure that he did this too.

Tristan is a wonderful reader and didn't need me to read to him. But I readily agreed, sensing that Charlotte's anxiety had affected him and he needed mothering.

The book that Tristan chose was from the Junie B. Jones series, *Junie B. Jones and her Big Fat Mouth*. I could identify with the character. Tristan's eyes drooped after the first few pages. I covered him with the blanket, kissed him on the forehead, and left the room leaving the night-light on.

Then I got a glass of orange juice and returned to my study. I had nearly finished re-reading my notes when Claudine phoned with "an emergency." She had to speak with me "now." I didn't mind this interruption. My mind had begun to wander and I needed a break. Nothing more completely removes you from your situation than advising a child about their "crisis."

"Kirsten is dating a boy who's a dirtbag and she asked me what I think of him. Should I lie or tell her?" Claudine asked, breathlessly.

Though both Kirsten and Claudine are eight, I didn't doubt what she was saying. Kids grow up more quickly nowadays. In my day, "dating" in elementary school involved walking down the hallway together and girls and boys sat separately in the lunchroom. But I wouldn't bet on how things are now. I took Claudine's question seriously.

"That's a big question. What don't you like about the boy?" I asked.

"You mean apart from him picking his nose and scratching his ass?" she asked, sarcastically.

I kept my cool though her tone had implied that she was speaking to a moron. Kirsten came from one of Greenwich's super-wealthy families. She had always been exquisitely dressed when I saw her. While it sounded like her "boyfriend" had issues, teenagers and adults often face the same problem: When do you tell the truth to a friend?

"OK," I said, pausing to give myself time to organize my thoughts.

"It sounds like Kirsten has doubts about this boy and wants your opinion of him. It you lie and he treats her badly, it would bite both of you down the road and you'd feel badly since you totally saw it coming. If I were you, I would tell her what you know for a fact or had seen with this boy. But don't tell her gossip about him since this may cause Kirsten to trust you less. Does this make sense?" I asked.

There was silence while Claudine digested my advice.

"Does it make sense?" I repeated.

"Yes," she said, calmly.

The rest of our conversation was ordinary: about her demanding teacher, and a birthday party that she would attend on Saturday. After hanging up, I felt refreshed and returned to studying.

An hour later, a call came from the building's front desk. A hand-delivered letter for Charlotte had been given to the doorman. He was bringing it right up.

Chapter 87

The letter was in a large manila envelope. I took it from the doorman. My smile disappeared as soon as the door was closed. I handled the envelope gingerly, as if it burned, and placed it on the dining room table.

I usually went to sleep when Charlotte wasn't likely to return until morning, leaving my bedroom door open lest Tristan call. That night I sprawled on the living room sofa. I would be awakened by her arrival. Opening the heavy locks on the apartment's door is a noisy business.

I sensed that the letter contained demands from the hacker and did not want her to be alone. Though Charlotte is far older than me, I knew that she would need someone to talk to.

In London a year earlier, Ivan told me that a person's worst enemy is panic. He said this while an explosive suicide vest had remained locked on my body. One of his military experts removed it. I owe Ivan my life.

I dozed off despite my intention to remain awake and study. In my dream, I had returned to a past event in Tokyo. I was tied to a table as the killer approached. I was to be tortured before dying. My eyes stared at the red-hot tip of the soldering iron in his advancing hand.

To increase my terror, my head had been locked into place. I was forced to watch a video of a previous victim being murdered and to hear her screams.

I screamed and jerked awake as Charlotte opened the door.

"Charlotte?" I called, in an unnaturally loud voice.

"Of course. Was that you?" she asked.

"It was just a dream," I replied.

"I wouldn't want one like it," she said, evenly.

I handed her the envelope as she entered the room.

"This came for you. It was hand-delivered," I said.

From their years of training, doctors have gained the ability to control their emotions. Charlotte opened the manila envelope and quickly scanned the two sheets it contained. Then she read them more carefully. She handed the pages to me.

"I need a drink," she said.

Chapter 88

Charlotte returned from the kitchen with a glass of orange juice. I was glad that it wasn't whiskey. Drinking and crises aren't a good mix.

The letter read as follows.

"Dear Charlotte.

"Though being strangers, I feel the right to address you by your first name since you are the mother of my son. I've noted in the playground that he is as handsome as his mother is beautiful.

"No, I haven't stalked you. I merely wanted to satisfy my curiosity as to whether Tristan resembles me, and he does. His name (which I like!) was easily gained. People talk and especially about the doctors that they favor.

"Why have I contacted you? Because, having achieved a doctorate in computer science and academic appointment, I want more from life. Like you, I have never married. The yearning that you experienced for children has now hit me and I wish contact with my son.

"I realize this letter will come as a shock and be experienced as an unwelcome intrusion into your family's order. But Tristan has a right to a father, and I possess rights to my son.

"I do not want to distress you. I suggest that we meet alone for dinner next Saturday evening. I have made reservations at Lincoln Ristorante at 7PM. It is at 142 West 65th Street, not far from your home, and the food is excellent. The restaurant has an open kitchen from which you can see the chefs working, and its glass walls give you a view of Lincoln Center. We can sit beside the outdoor reflecting pool if you prefer. The crowd tends to be older and quieter, and this is a blessing.

"You will doubtless check up on me, as you should. What you find will confirm my education and professional status. It will also reveal my past legal problems though I have never been properly convicted of any crime. There are no charges against me, and the prosecutor will not seek a new trial. From a legal standpoint, I am as free as you.

"I look forward to our meeting. If the time is inconvenient, please call and we can schedule another. Tristan—and his mother—are both cherished by me and I do not want to cause either of you distress.

"With my sincerest, best wishes,"

Charlotte had been silently drinking her juice as I read.

"He's slippery, all right. He'll want money to go away," I said.

"Yes, but I don't have much," Charlotte said.

I stared, and she sensed my disbelief. To live in a three-bedroom apartment in a doorman building overlooking Central Park requires big bucks in

Manhattan. My eyes turned to the four-thousand dollar bag draped on the chair beside me.

"Huge student loans got me through medical school and residency. This apartment carries a large variable rate mortgage which continually increases, and Tristan's private school tuition could pay for another apartment. I have a medical school academic appointment and most of my patients' fees go to the university. Not all doctors are rich.

"And in case you're wondering, the bag that you admire was a gift from a grateful patient, a partner in a law firm. For all I know, it may have been re-gifted."

"I'm sorry. I didn't mean to doubt you," I said.

"Apology accepted. Many City doctors were once rich but not now. Managed care has fixed fees, Manhattan office rents are exorbitant, and malpractice insurance rates are sky-high, particularly for obstetricians."

Chapter 89

I looked down at the letter that I was holding and something occurred to me.

"How are you supposed to recognize or contact him?" I asked.

"I don't know."

I looked in the large manila envelope. At its bottom lay a small photograph of a handsome man. There could be little doubt that he was Tristan's father. On the back of the photo was written: "blue blazer, tan slacks, polo shirt," and a phone number. I handed the photo to Charlotte.

"He's thought of everything," I said.

"Yes," she replied, in a low voice.

Charlotte looked defeated. You don't want that appearance when you're battling a monster, I thought.

"Forgive me if I'm forgetting my place but you shouldn't meet him alone. He's too dangerous," I said, in a measured voice.

I had met brutes and knew what I was talking about.

"He said that I should be alone and that we could sit outside. What can happen?" Charlotte asked, as if clinging to a ray of hope.

"Nothing, at the restaurant. But what if he drugs your drink? Who would involve themselves as he helped you to stagger away? You'll feel safer if you have someone watching your back. Your lawyer should be able to arrange this. If he can't, Ivan should be able to help. He watched over me while I was in London."

"Why did you need protection?" Charlotte asked.

"My English dad became famous. It's a long story," I said, briefly.

I wanted to drop the subject. If Charlotte knew what happened in London, she might never leave her apartment.

"Thank you. I'll call the lawyer in the morning. You'd better get to bed," Charlotte said, now sounding more her normal self.

You've done a good job, I told myself, as I crawled into bed. I hope you do as well on the exam.

The next evening, while eating in the campus cafeteria, both Missy and I felt that we had aced the test. I was feeling good until a familiar worry arose. Missy's pregnancy was no longer a campus issue but unfamiliar students would still stop at our table and ask how she is— meaning how her baby is. She would return their smile, pat her belly, and both would grin. This is part of being pregnant, I told myself.

"How *really* are you?" I asked Missy, after one such encounter.

Margaret of Greenwich

"The baby is fine but I can't stop thinking about Odis. I *know* that he's alive," she replied sadly.

She still holds that belief, I told myself, and my worry about her deepened. The last thing that a newborn needs is an irrational mother!

Chapter 90

The days seemed to pass more quickly as the date for Charlotte's meeting approached. It takes time for depression to be overcome and time wasn't what she had. To cope with the stress, Charlotte had occupied herself with hospital work. Thus, I was babysitting Tristan during nearly the entire week.

Tristan noticed the change in his mother and her replies to his questions hadn't satisfied him.

"Mom looks sad. Is she alright?" he asked me, when we were alone.

"Doctors worry about their patients. She'll soon be her usual self," I replied, and hugged him.

Tristan stared at me but didn't say anything. Neither of us believed my reply.

But Charlotte *could not* tell Tristan what was happening. A child must feel safe to survive, not have to fear a lurking monster.

That Saturday, Charlotte obsessed what to wear.

"Make it plain, not sexy, and definitely not expensive," I suggested, and she agreed.

The private detective that she had hired arrived at 6PM and instructed her.

"I'll be at the restaurant's bar, watching the entrance. I won't book a table until you've chosen. Don't look at me or even think about me. And don't, under any circumstances, accompany him anywhere.

"I'll intervene if I feel the situation is getting out of hand, I'll introduce myself as being your old friend, Charlie Havens, a past administrator of Harlem Hospital where you've consulted. Your job is to be courteous but not friendly, and to discover what he wants without agreeing to anything. Do you have any questions?"

Charlotte didn't. She left the apartment at 6:30PM. The detective had left earlier.

I tried to read while awaiting her return but couldn't concentrate. I sensed that Charlotte was meeting this challenge wrong. She hoped to reason with a monster and this never works.

If given a choice of whether to tickle a crocodile's head or shoot it, I'd always pull the trigger. Even in fairy tales, monsters must be destroyed. How could Charlotte be so wrong? I asked myself, though I understood.

Living in an ordered, lawful society deadens our ingrained, reptilian instinct that insures survival. I must remind Charlotte of this, I told myself.

People read about killers but can't believe that they will impact their lives—until they do. Only the meanest and sneakiest and toughest victims survive. I had survived. I vowed that Charlotte and Tristan would survive though I didn't yet know how.

My mother once told me that everyone has a right to fail. I won't fail with Charlotte and Tristan, I told myself. *Not with them*, I repeated, and took a deep breath.

You need only experience battle once to recognize its sound. I could hear the shells crashing, loud and clear.

Chapter 91

Charlotte returned home a little before nine. She was accompanied by the detective. He entered with her. She permitted him to inspect the apartment for danger before leaving.

"Tristan?" she asked me.

"He's fine but is worrying about you. He was sleeping a few minutes ago," I said.

Charlotte nodded, seated herself on the sofa, and took off her shoes. Then she held her face in her hands and began sobbing.

"What does he want?" I asked, softly, when her tears subsided.

"A million dollars to start, then ten-thousand dollars a month until Tristan turns eighteen," she replied.

"You don't have that kind of money?" I asked.

"*No way*, and I couldn't raise it."

"You told him this."

"Of course. Oh, he was charming and listened and made no threats. He just spoke of the pain that lacking contact with his son causes him and how his lawyer was hungering to go into court to remedy this. It would be a landmark case, his lawyer had assured him. It would destroy Tristan and me!"

I let silence descend over us for a half-minute. It is a sensitive matter for a teenager to give advice to an adult but I felt that someone had to tell her what I was about to say. If her lawyer hadn't done this it would have to be me.

"You're approaching him wrong," I said.

Charlotte stared, not with the look of anger that I had feared but with a glimpse of hope.

"You can't trust him. He's a monster and you destroy monsters, you don't feed them. Once you pay him, he'll soon want more. Maybe insist on having sex with you." I said.

"You're right but what choice do I have?" Charlotte asked, with a look of revulsion on her face.

"I don't know. My dad is a great lawyer and knows many people. I'll call him. When does he want an answer?"

"Within two weeks. After that, his lawyer goes into court, he said."

"I'll phone my dad in the morning," I said.

On that note we both went to sleep.

Chapter 92

We went to church the next day though Charlotte had lost most of her religious leanings. She, like many others, viewed church attendance as a social occasion. A place to meet congenial families and arrange play dates for Tristan. "I feel more comfortable there than fixing meetups with mothers online," she had told me.

Missy begged off joining us. "Not with *my* bladder," she said, using the excuse that is readily accepted by every mother. So it was just the three of us.

Tristan was calm throughout the long service. This surprised me until I noticed the tiny video game in his hand. He had constructed it with his Raspberry Pi. I stared down and he looked up. We both smiled. Religious services aren't intended to be fun.

Following every Mormon service are groups segregated by age and sex. Charlotte remained for them but I left, saying that I had to study. That was true but it was mostly thinking that I had to do.

I had told Charlotte that I would ask my dad for advice. I said this to give her hope but had no intention of doing it. I already knew what he would say: once you get into court, all bets are off. A judge may be wise or opinionated and gaining justice is far from certain. Hearing these facts wouldn't lift anyone's mood.

Being unsure what to do, I returned to the dorm and spent the next nine hours studying. Charlotte had worked obsessively to avoid thinking about her problem and I studied zealously to do the same.

It was dark when I left the dorm for a break. I carried my English father's walking stick. It had protected me in London and gave me a feeling of security while walking the streets at night.

I had often gone running when facing a problem but City streets aren't suited for this. Instead, I walked with a quick, determined step, from the dormitory across to Riverside Drive and into the park.

I walked along the dark, deserted pathway. I planned to return to the bright lights of Broadway at the 96th Street exit. While walking, I suddenly realized what I was doing. I felt rage at what was happening and hoped to encounter a mugger. I wanted to strike out, smash him with my walking stick as I had the London thug. But no robber appeared.

There comes a moment with every problem when things come together and understanding floods over you. You are intently focused and know what must be done. I suddenly *knew* yet didn't want to do it. But I had vowed that Charlotte and Tristan would be saved. I would not fail.

I sat on a park bench and lay the walking stick beside me. I took my iPhone from my jacket and brought up the long unused number. My breathing slowed and calm returned as the ringing began.

Chapter 93

The number that I dialed had a European area code. I had been told to use it if ever I needed help.

There were odd sounds on the line before the call was answered. A woman with a clipped English accent repeated the telephone number that I had called. I told her who I was and who I wanted to speak with and she asked me to hold on. There were more sounds on the line before I heard the familiar voice.

"I need help," I said, quickly.

"Are you in danger?"

"No, but others are."

"Where are you?"

I told him and there was a momentary silence before he instructed me where to go and who to ask for.

"You will be safe. I must complete some work and will arrive shortly."

He immediately disconnected. I called for an Uber taxi using the account that Charlotte had opened for me. I felt this would be proper since my trip concerned her.

I had never been to the area of Manhattan where I was going. Nevertheless, I felt the sense of relief that comes after a tough decision is made. I felt confident that things would turn out OK. Not that night but soon.

Traffic was heavy and it took nearly a half hour to reach the restaurant. Despite the late hour, the streets were packed. The headwaiter wore traditional Chinese garb. I told him my name and who I was meeting. He said that the gentleman had not yet arrived but that a private room had been reserved.

The room was one flight up at the back of a long hallway. A tall, powerfully built, Chinese man stood at the door. His face was a mask of death where nothing lived except the eyes. He had a sharp nose and outward turning ear lobes. His mouth was a thin slit. I saw a large pistol in his waistband when he bowed upon my arrival. He opened the door.

Unlike the sharply colored décor downstairs, this room's furnishings were subdued. It resembled an English drawing room. A sofa was surrounded by three club chairs. Paintings of horseback riders and gardens hung from the walls.

In one corner was a small dining room table surrounded by four well-padded chairs. The windows were curtained. When I looked out, I found that they were locked and gated. Though a guest, I was also a prisoner.

Menus lay on the table and the headwaiter asked if I wished to order. I declined, stating that I would wait for my companion. He left and I was alone. I sat on the sofa, took a pen and pad from my backpack, and began writing.

As with most people, my handwriting has deteriorated in these days when nearly everything is typed. I took pains to write clearly.

The writing went quicker than I had expected. I read my production repeatedly. It's persuasive but is it convincing enough? I asked myself.

I replaced the pen and pad in my backpack, sprawled, and soon dozed off. I awoke to a touch on my shoulder.

"I'm sorry that I was delayed. When did you last eat?"

"So long ago that I can barely remember," I replied, sleepily.

"Is the danger that you spoke of immediate?"

"No," I replied.

"We'll eat first. Decisions are best made on a full stomach," Ivan said.

Chapter 94

Ivan ordered for both of us. I've eaten with his family often and he knows what I like.

We had Spicy Yellow Tail Yu Sheng (smoked chili and pineapple), Vegetable Rice, and Salt & Pepper Black Bass made with Ginger and Red Sauce. I drank water and chose Fortune Cookies for dessert, feeling that a good prediction couldn't hurt the situation. But after reading them I wasn't sure what was foretold.

My fortune cookie read, "Be on the lookout for coming events. They cast their shadows beforehand." Ivan's fortune cookie read, "Meeting adversity well is the source of your strength." After eating, we left the table, sat on the sofa, and got down to business.

I told Ivan of Tristan's birth through artificial insemination, and of his notorious criminal father who was blackmailing Charlotte. I also told him what my lawyer-father had said: that court decisions are unpredictable.

Ivan crossed his legs and sprawled as I spoke. He looked down as if he were half-asleep but I knew he was listening closely. When I finished, he turned toward me and spoke.

"Charlotte has been kind to Missy. She will likely become part of our family and family is very important to Russians. That man will never stop hounding Charlotte. I can't let that happen," he said.

"He must be stopped," I agreed.

I told Ivan my idea and handed him what I had written. He read the sheets slowly. Then he gave me a long, hard stare before speaking.

"What must be done will be done. None could doubt that you are Vladimir's daughter. You've done him proud," he said, as he folded and placed the sheets into his pocket.

"I don't feel proud," I said.

"Tristan's father is a snake. When a snake attacks, there is only one way to deal with it," Ivan said.

"Yes, but I still feel badly."

"That is because you are a moral person. Do you have a mirror?" Ivan asked.

When I said that I did, he asked me to take it out and look into it. Though being puzzled, I did so.

"In the mirror you see a girl who distinguishes good from evil. One who believes so strongly in justice that she would sacrifice for the sake of her principles. Is this a fair picture of you?"

"I never wanted to be a saint," I replied.

"Maybe not, but your motives are saintly. You are on the side of the angels and will sleep well tonight. Come, I'll drive you home," Ivan said.

He was right. That night I slept a deep, dreamless sleep, as if I were being held aloft by angels.

Chapter 95

We could do nothing but wait. Charlotte continued working fanatically, trying to avoid awareness of the crisis enveloping her life. Tristan remained worried about his mother and I spent much of that week reassuring him.

Though feeling confident that Ivan would succeed, there could be no certainty. Vladimir once said that the most important military principle is that the first person to shoot will kill the other. Tristan's father had fired the first shot. Was Charlotte's cause hopeless from the start? We didn't yet know.

I tried to keep myself occupied. I was certain that I had studied enough for my remaining exams but continued studying. You can never do too much studying, I told myself.

During breaks, and when Tristan wasn't busy creating gadgets with his Raspberry Pi, we watched TV. Yes, even genius children watch TV though the shows that Tristan likes aren't only those that characterize kids his age.

What we watched on Nick at Night were reruns of a long ago TV hit, *Alfred Hitchcock Presents*. Hitchcock is one of Melody's favorite movie directors and, being a student of films, her opinion counts. Any of the more than fifty movies that he made is worth viewing. Try *North by Northwest*, *Shadow of a Doubt*, and *Rear Window*, which I've already mentioned. You'll love them.

Margaret of Greenwich

Tristan enjoys shows with twisty plots. In one of them, a wife is attacked and left traumatized. She and her husband drive through town. She points out the assailant and her husband kills him. Later, she identifies another man as the attacker and it is learned that the woman has mental problems.

In another show, two cowboys meet in a bar and threaten a shoot-out. The owner fails to calm them but convinces them to shoot at each other only when the clock strikes. When the clock mysteriously stops, the cowboys take it as a sign from God and leave the bar peacefully.

I breathed deeply at the close of this story. A sign from God is what we're hoping for, I told myself. It arrived the next day, in the appearance of a gray-haired, middle-aged man.

Chapter 96

The man arrived at Charlotte's apartment at a little after 10AM. He had told the doorman that he was Horace Burroughs, an attorney.

Charlotte wasn't dressed when she opened the door. She was without makeup and wore a robe over her pajamas. I heard her return home at seven so she couldn't have had more than several hours sleep. She looked exhausted.

Mr. Burroughs gave Charlotte his business card and quickly explained why he had come.

"I'm the attorney for Tristan's father. I received a letter from him yesterday and will file it with the Court today. It affects his case and I considered it likely that you would want to see it at once. I've made a copy for you."

Mr. Burroughs removed an envelope from his briefcase and handed it to Charlotte. She opened it slowly. Tears appeared as she read the letter. Mr. Burroughs looked embarrassed.

"I'll leave now. I'm sure that you're very busy. Feel free to call me if you have any questions," he said.

When the door was closed and locked, Charlotte read the letter to me.

"Dear Charlotte,

"Perhaps the only advantage of aging is that one becomes capable of viewing their life with greater maturity. When donating sperm as a penniless student, I did it solely for the money and had no desire for children. While this changed, I now realize that parenting demands more than the desire. Tristan is developing into a commendable youth and I have nothing to contribute to his life. Indeed, my intrusion might well harm him.

"Thus, I herewith renounce all claim to visitation or custody of my son, Tristan. I have decided to leave New York and live under a new identity. I will try to make amends for the regrettable events in my life. I wish you and my son well."

"It's a noble letter. I would never have expected it of him," Charlotte said.

Nor would I and that's why I wrote it, I told myself, with more than a hint of pride.

Chapter 97

As soon as Charlotte left the room, I went to my bedroom, closed the door, and called Ivan.

"A lawyer just left. Charlotte's problem is over," I said.

"Yes, I expected that it would be," he replied smoothly.

"You persuaded Tristan's father?"

"It took convincing but he eventually agreed."

"What if he changes his mind?"

"That's not possible. But if you dine at the restaurant where we ate..."

"Yes?"

"I would avoid the meat dishes," Ivan said.

"Thank you," I murmured softly, before hanging up.

I couldn't help wondering why the lawyer had felt the need to personally deliver the letter to Charlotte. Perhaps he felt uncomfortable at the legal duties he had undertaken, I mused.

Now there's just Missy's childbirth to worry about and we're home free, I told myself.

Tristan immediately noticed the change in his mother.

"She's not sad," he told me, later that morning.

"Nope. Grownups get their ups and downs just like kids," I said.

Tristan nodded. His worry was gone.

Charlotte immediately cut back her hospital hours so I saw less of Tristan during the remaining weeks of the school term. Missy's delivery went well and Cordelia was a bouncing eight pounds, four ounces. Everyone was thrilled.

After giving birth, Missy and Cordelia moved into Charlotte's apartment. Tristan now had the sister he wanted. I lost use of the spare bedroom and most of my babysitting hours but didn't mind. Reliable, experienced babysitters are much in demand by wealthy Manhattan couples and I quickly gained new clients.

Having begun to consider my first year at Barnard, I came to view myself as being more a camera than a participant. The principal actors had been Missy and Charlotte and Tristan, with supporting roles played by Ivan and Artur and Randy and Clarence.

Still, my role had been crucial even if I hadn't been a starring player. But I hadn't been a mere recorder since cameras are passive. Submitting to evil or ignoring a cry for help was never my style.

The dorm had nearly emptied for the summer when Jill banged on my door. Though I recognized her, we hadn't been friends.

"Can I talk to you?" she asked, sobbing.

Without waiting for my response, Jill poured out her story.

"My boyfriend and I had planned to spend the summer at my parents' house on Fire Island and to rent an apartment near campus for the fall. He just dropped me and I don't know why," she moaned.

"Did you ask him?"

"*Of course I asked him* but I didn't get an answer. He just said that he'd been unhappy."

"How long were you dating?" I asked.

"Two months."

"Was he your first lover?"

"No, I had two boyfriends in high school but I ended those relationships. Why did he drop me? I need closure."

I had no idea why Jill's boyfriend dropped her. As I remembered, she was prone to making cutting remarks which she considered cute but annoyed others. This might have been why her boyfriend broke up with her. Still, she had asked for my help and I knew *this* explanation very definitely wasn't what she wanted to hear.

"OK. It beats me what could have happened between the two of you and possibly your boyfriend isn't sure either. Maybe he wasn't ready for a deep relationship and this awareness suddenly hit him. But you had a good experience and that's what's important," I said.

"What was good about it?" Jill asked, wiping her eyes.

"You've learned that you're capable of loving deeply. Having done so once, you can do it again," I replied.

Jill hugged me, thanked me, and left. My advice seemed to work. I next saw Jill two days later. She smiled and waved as we passed each other on Broadway. She was locked arm-in-arm with a man and looked happy.

By late June my life had turned peaceful and untroubled. Would some new event add to this year's turmoil? I wondered, Then they did, not one event but two. And, though incredible, they were unquestionably true.

Chapter 98

At the end of term, Erika suggested that we hold a party to celebrate the completion of our first year at college. She was a Randy's classmate at Yale and had casually kept tabs on him for me. Not that I didn't trust him but as President Reagan had said about a far more important matter: trust but verify.

Being a billionaire's daughter, Erika's home is far larger than any of ours. Their house has sixteen bedrooms and thirteen bathrooms. She offered to hold the party there. Her father, a widower, wouldn't object, she said. He welcomes weekend visitors.

Almost everyone that we knew would be invited. These included: my biological father and mother and grandmother; my adoptive parents and sisters; Randy and his parents and baby sister; Missy and her baby and family; Artur and his parents; Vladimir and Ulrika and their baby daughter; and more.

A week later, Missy, Cordelia, and Artur and I sat on a bench outside Central Park. Despite the gorgeous day, Missy remained depressed. She couldn't stop thinking about Odis.

"He must be dead. I received no charm on my birthday yesterday," she said, sadly.

"But your love for him will never die. Love is forever," I said, and Missy nodded.

At just that moment a black sedan parked opposite us though the space was labelled "No Parking." Courtesy is becoming rarer in big cities, I thought.

Three men exited the car. Two were dressed in suits while the third wore a stiff, round, flat-topped white cap and uniform. He was bearded, and I saw that his name tag read Delacroix. He stood before Missy and stared into her face. The other men flanked him from several paces back.

Artur sensed danger and gripped Cordelia more tightly. He stiffened as the uniformed man reached into his pocket. But it wasn't a gun or a knife that he removed but something tiny. Missy stared up at him with a puzzled look on her face.

"Can I help you?" she asked, coolly.

"My plane was delayed. I'm sorry your gift is late," he said, dropping what he had been holding into her lap.

It was a Pandora Heart Silver Dangle charm. Missy stared at it uncomprehendingly before grasping its meaning. She studied the man's face.

"Am I that different, Missy?" he asked, softly.

At these words, Missy sprang from the bench. Her voice overcame the loud traffic noise.

"Odis," she screamed, throwing herself into his arms.

Chapter 99

Missy sobbed and clung to Odis, being reluctant to let him go. When they finally disengaged, I suggested that we return to Charlotte's apartment and this was agreed. Odis introduced the men as being FBI agents who were assigned to protect him. We readily accepted this unusual explanation. His ten year absence could have caused just about anything.

Once in the apartment, I explained the situation to Charlotte. Missy had already told her of Odis' disappearance. All stood around, not knowing where to begin. To ease the situation, I brought yoghurt dip and crackers and bottles of water and juice packs from the kitchen.

After seating ourselves in the living room, the FBI agents stared at Tristan.

"Tristan is only seven but he's a genius," Charlotte said, and he remained in the room.

For all we knew, Tristan's comments might be the most intelligent.

"I had no choice. I had to leave to try to save myself and our family," Odis began, taking a sip of water before continuing.

"I was always fascinated by computers and Harvard's Computer Science department was like a toy store for me. I took exams to skip the basic courses. My first computer class was a small advanced one. The professor suggested that I choose a project and computers are best at just one thing."

"Engineers call it pattern recognition but computer scientists call it machine learning," Tristan burst out.

"I told you Tristan is a genius. You might consider hiring him," Charlotte said proudly, as the FBI agents stared. We didn't, being used to Tristan's ways.

"Yes, pattern recognition. There had been murders in the Boston area and I decided to study the type of crime and where and when it happened. Then, this was new though many police departments do it now.

"My teacher became intrigued. He suggested that I expand my research to cover a nation. Because the United States is large and our statistics were sketchy, I chose France. Their data was more complete and I'm fluent in French, having studied it since grade school.

"Mind you, I was doing this for a grade. I didn't expect anything serious to come of it. I mean, I was an eighteen-year-old college kid. What could happen?" Odis asked rhetorically.

"Those are famous last words," I burst out, having often said them after becoming involved in situations that I should have avoided.

"Just so," Odis said, and he continued his story.

Chapter 100

"My professor was excited about my project. 'You'll get a book out of it,' he predicted. But the more work that I did, the harder it became. Studying crime isn't easy since many crimes aren't reported to the police: those involving children, or with domestic violence when it is considered better to arrest the man than the woman because she has kids to care for despite both parties being equally to blame.

"When a person is asked if they are the victim of crime without needing to provide supporting evidence, it is the person's opinion that a crime occurred, or even their understanding of what constitutes a crime, that is being measured.

"There are other factors too. Having to make an insurance claim or to require medical aid tend increase the level of reporting. The inconvenience of reporting and the involvement of lovers tend to decrease it. Car thefts are usually reported because this is needed to file an insurance claim but family violence, family child abuse, and sexual offenses often aren't reported because of the intimate relationships involved and embarrassment.

"A British study found that the national average of under-recording of crime was nineteen percent, over eight-hundred-thousand crimes each year.

"Neither my professor nor I knew this when I began my study. Once we did, he suggested that a smaller geographic area would more be likely to have accurate statistics. I didn't know which to choose so I closed my eyes, hoped for the best, and stuck a pin in a map of

France. My pin hit the island of Corsica, and that's when my real problems began," Odis said, stopping to take another sip of water.

I looked at the others. Their faces held the same astonishment as mine. Odis' story was *really* something though none of us should have been surprised: a ten year disappearance must have a powerful motive. But how could a college class project have created it? I asked myself, before speaking this question aloud.

"Crime or not, you were just studying statistics not people. How could playing around with numbers cause you trouble?" I asked.

Odis smiled, and shook his head.

"Well, that wasn't all that I did since I soon became curious. What do they say about curiosity, Tristan?"

"Curiosity killed the cat," Tristan replied happily.

He was glad to be taken seriously, to be accepted a member of this adult group.

"*Right,* and it nearly got me killed," Odis said, with a smile.

Despite his smile, Odis' tone had been dark, not comical.

Chapter 101

We peered intently at Odis. His story gripped us so strongly that we would have resented interruption but none came. There was no knock on the door or phone call. Nothing.

Odis resembles Randy in their telling of stories. Both heighten suspense by pausing at the most exciting moments. Then, Odis sipped water and who would criticize this action? It would be like demanding of a stutterer that they speak more quickly.

"It began when I tried to improve my results by getting better data. The numbers that police provide are incomplete and late in coming, sometimes years after the fact. My project was due in months and I needed good numbers *then*."

While Odis took another sip of water, Tristan burst out, with a big grin, "You hacked for them."

Tristan was sitting beside Odis on the sofa. Odis reached over and ruffled Tristan's hair.

"Why have you been hiding this genius?" he asked, with a grin that matched Tristan's.

Tristan snuggled close, Odis put his arm around him, and this seemed to relax both.

"Let's just say that I got the numbers I needed," Odis said, looking toward the FBI agents.

"While looking at them I became interested in the patterning of crimes. The street crimes—pickpocketing, small theft—were scattered all over the island. This made sense since Corsica is one of the poorest regions of France. Yet according to public records, some people were living very well. They had mansions and owned cars that we can only dream about.

"Then I remembered Corsica's notorious reputation. There are no large businesses on poverty stricken Corsica so the wealthy must be criminals, I concluded. Corsica is their home and they're committing crimes elsewhere. I tried to discover who *they* were and what *they* did.

"My professor didn't know any of this. I told him only that my project was progressing. Simply getting an 'A' no longer interested me. I had discovered a puzzle and intended to solve it."

"I solve puzzles too," Tristan piped up.

"My new friend and helper," Odis said, ruffling his hair again.

"My first information came from old French newspapers. They told of sensational crimes, like the escape of gangsters from a prison near Bastia which is the second largest city on Corsica. A fake fax had been sent ordering their release. Other stories described the killings of members of Corsican gangs. The largest of these is Brise de Mer. It's named after a Bastia café where the members had held meetings thirty years before. Brise de Mer means *Sea Breeze*.

"That group became my focus. I saw my research as having greater possibility than the dull, statistics-ridden book that my professor hoped for. I wanted to write a best-seller that could be turned into a hit movie like *The Godfather*. It already had a great title, *Sea*

Breeze, and a great plot: young computer student battles crime. I loved the first *Hulk* movie and maybe identified with him. God, was I dumb!"

Chapter 102

"I assumed that the richest people on Corsica would have the most expensive homes. I obtained the names of their owners from housing records, and then information about businesses that they were involved with. I also got their banking records. The banks' computer security was so poor that I could have stolen their money too but I didn't.

"The other facts that I wanted weren't public knowledge. Crooks don't use checking accounts. They launder money and have shell corporations in Luxembourg and elsewhere. I had to do more."

Odis took another sip of water as we waited. None of us had touched our refreshments since he began speaking.

"My roommate was fascinated by phones, the primitive ones of ten years ago. You might even say that he was a budding Steve Jobs. Jobs began his career making phreaking phone boxes, gadgets which enabled people to make free calls.

"I told my friend what I wanted to do. He taught me how to do it. It didn't take long to learn since digital phones are basically computers. I began listening in on the crime boss' phone calls though not as many as I would have liked since I didn't have that much time. I had classes to attend and homework to do.

"Of course, they spoke in coded terms. You don't ask someone over the phone how a robbery or murder went. But I got their meaning though as evidence it would never have held up in court.

"Computer nerd battles deadly criminals. You can't beat that for a movie plot, can you?"

None of us replied to Odis' rhetorical question. We awaited his answer.

"Yes, you can–if he nearly gets killed!" Odis said, before taking another sip of water.

"I'd been investigating as if it were a video game. In it, a player is slain before the game begins anew with them being OK. Real life isn't like that. This gang was murdering and robbing throughout Europe. They owned businesses in Africa and America and Latin America. They'd operated for decades and killed people who got in their way.

"I'm just a college kid, half a world away in Boston. They wouldn't harm me, I told myself. And I really believed it until they came after me."

Chapter 103

I straightened up. What Odis had said, "Until they came after me," didn't have a good ring.

"I hadn't thought of the danger that my research placed me in though I should have. I mean, when you're doing something nasty to someone shouldn't you expect their reaction?"

None of us answered this rhetorical question. Tristan might have but he lay relaxed against Odis' shoulder, thinking whatever thoughts that genius seven-year-olds have.

"I later realized that their computer people hadn't been entirely dumb. They must have had traceback software on their computers. I had been using the college's Wi-Fi for my official project but was being honest and using my personal Wi-Fi for the rest. This wasn't smart but, like they say, beginners are learners.

"Even after their first attempt to kidnap me, I didn't realize what was happening. I was crossing a street at night and two guys jumped from a van. Dumb luck saved me when a patrol car passed us. I still have a scar from where my arm hit the pavement."

Odis rolled up his sleeve to reveal the mark though this hadn't been necessary. None of us doubted his story.

"Then they tried to drug me at a local hangout. They put something in the drink directly in front of me. But it wasn't mine and the guy who drank it got dizzy and fell and his friends hustled him away.

"*That* got me thinking. One such incident might be chance but two? I don't believe in coincidence for things like that. A voice in my head told me to run. That night I maxed out my cash at an ATM, filled the gas tank, and went to Denny's to think.

"I had been studying there and gotten friendly with a waitress. Kaley was also a student. She studied forensic science at the community college and worked part-time at Denny's. There were few customers around and we got to talking. She saw that I was upset and said that she was getting off in a half-hour. We could meet and talk if I wanted, and I did.

"We talked in McDonalds for hours but there was nothing romantic about it. She already had a boyfriend. He was in the military, the Special Forces, where her dad was a Colonel.

"I told her everything and she took my fear seriously. Much more than the police who would have brushed me off as a crazy teenager. Kaley really got into my situation. She said that I had to disappear and make it look like I was dead. She put together the plan that saved my life."

Chapter 104

Odis took another sip of water. He got up to stretch and Tristan imitated him. The rest of us sat riveted in our seats. It was as if we were listening to the story that we had seen in so many movies: a guy on the run from the mob. Except that Odis had been eighteen and until leaving for college, had never lived apart from his family.

Odis sat down, Tristan snuggled close and Odis placed his arm around him. Should Tristan be hearing this story? I asked myself. You're not his mother and what do you know about genius kids anyway, my mind instantly replied.

"Kaley insisted that I and my family would be safe only if I were believed to be dead. I knew she was right."

My question burst out.

"You were just a college freshman. How did you feel that night?" I asked.

Odis turned toward me. There was a moment before he replied.

"I felt as if I held a pistol to my head. I didn't leave America just to save myself. My curiosity had taken on an almost religious passion. I wanted to make this dark world a little brighter by removing from it an evil that delighted in murder, and especially in killing the families of their enemies. If I failed—if Missy and my family were killed—my life would be over too."

Odis returned to his story.

"'The police will need your blood, DNA, and ID to confirm your death. Two should be enough but we'll give them all three,' Kaley said. She was licensed as a phlebotomist and had equipment at home so taking my blood was no problem."

"Like Dracula," Tristan said, with a sly grin.

"Well, not quite," Odis replied, turning toward him. "A phlebotomist is a person who draws blood for medical tests," Odis explained.

"We smeared my blood in my car. We removed the money and credit cards from my wallet and placed it under the seat. We left the car unlocked, with its key in the ignition, in a no-parking zone.

"We were sure that the car would be ticketed and towed. The police would investigate and I'd be described as the victim of another tragic crime. Those seeking me would end their search. Unfortunately, that's not what happened. What's the biggest mistake that a crook can make?" Odis asked.

It was as if he had become a teacher taking charge of his classroom. An FBI agent shifted in his seat and looked around. He spoke when a reply didn't come. "Their biggest mistake is believing they control everything," he said.

Odis nodded agreement, and continued telling his story.

Chapter 105

"Kaley said I needed toughening up and that the military was the best place to get it. 'You'll be safe there too.' But where could I get it? I couldn't enlist in the American army. The phony ID that I was using wouldn't pass with them.

"'The Foreign Legion is perfect for you. I saw a movie about it. They take everyone and you already speak French,'" Kaley said.

"That was all that we knew about the Foreign Legion, what she remembered from a movie. Though when we checked on the Internet, it turned out that she was right. My only problem was how to join since they recruited only in France.

"'You're going to Paris,' Kaley said, and that's what I did. On the way to Kennedy Airport I asked myself why I was letting Kaley boss me around. Then I realized that I had always been that way with older girls. They tended to mother me and I was apt to follow their advice. We parted at the airport and I promised to keep in touch."

Now Odis turned toward Missy.

"It was Kaley who sent you the birthday charm each year using a re-mailing service. I told her that I'd deliver this year's gift in person," Odis said.

"You needed a passport to travel. Whose did you use?" an FBI man asked.

"Let's just say that a friend who I resembled lent me theirs. Kaley said that if a passport photo and its holder is of the same race and hair color and has a beard or doesn't, officials don't look further. I mailed back his passport later.

"Enlisting in the Foreign Legion isn't like in the movies since they do check to see if you're wanted by the police. I was able to run two miles in under ten minutes which is their first physical test. I also did the required four pull-ups, had good vision, and enough of my teeth. I looked healthier than most of the other recruits. They were pretty thin.

"Military life involves a lot of waiting around. During the first week the boredom almost drove me crazy. I thought of dropping out. Claiming that I had just gotten out of a mental hospital and hustling back to America. That was until I lucked out.

"I did so well on the IQ test that the doctor questioned me. I told him of my skill with computers and he called in his boss. He became excited and I wound up as part of the one-percent of Legionnaires that support the military. After Basic Training, I was assigned to an air-conditioned Computer Support office instead of an insect-ridden tropical base," Odis said.

Chapter 106

The man who had appeared to be the senior FBI agent looked meaningfully at his watch. Then he stared at Odis who picked up the hint.

"We have to get going so I'll sum up quickly," Odis said. "I used the military's mainframe to gain information on the gang and the corrupt politicians that supported them. But it took me years since their security kept improving. I copied the incriminating files onto USB thumb drives that I gave to the FBI liaison in Paris. They had some authority since several of the crimes were committed in America. The American Ambassador spoke with the French government and I was released from the remaining months of my second five-year enlistment. It was important that I return to America quickly."

Odis paused to take a sip of water. I sensed that there was yet another surprising element in his story and played along.

"Why was that?" I asked, innocently.

"My wife wanted our child to be born in America," he said, with a big grin.

"*Odis!*" Missy screamed, and flung herself into his arms for the second time that day.

The adults grinned but Tristan seemed puzzled by this display of emotion. Even genius kids can't understand some things, I told myself.

We sat around talking after Odis and his bodyguards left. One of them gave Missy his business card and said that Odis could be contacted through him. He said that Odis would be busy helping government lawyers, and that his wife was being held in protective custody too.

"I wonder what she's like. Odis didn't say whether she's French or American," Missy said.

"She's probably American. Why else would she insist on having her baby born here?" Charlotte asked.

I wasn't so sure. I had read stories on Google News about foreigners who travel to the USA to give birth so their child would have American citizenship. Wouldn't Odis' child gain this automatically by nature of their father being American? I asked. None of us knew the answer but there was one point on which everyone agreed.

"They *must* come to Erika's party!" Missy insisted.

Chapter 107

Erika's party was everything that you could hope for. It would have made the social column in the local paper if Odis hadn't been under FBI protection. Only after he threatened to stop cooperating did the FBI allow him to attend. But they could not fault the estate's security. It is surrounded by an eight foot, glass shard topped wall, and has shotgun toting, retired Russian Special Forces sentries roaming the grounds on a 24/7 basis. Other guards, carrying pistols, wander indoors.

Guests came from Charleston and London and Berlin. Erika's forty million dollar house is huge so space is never a problem. The resident cook handled most of the meals except for a few special items: Russian Osetra Caviar (buckwheat blinis, lemon-crème fraiche) for Vladimir, and *pupcakes* (cupcakes with the face of owls, pandas, or puppies) for the children from Greenwich's St. Moritz Bakery.

The kids played with Erika's childhood toys and games while the grownups talked. Odis introduced us to his very pregnant, American wife, Constance.

The party—it was really a re-bonding—lasted three days though Odis and his wife had to leave on the second day. Surprisingly, since our house is just a few miles away, my parents stayed over too. The teenagers talked most of the night, like at a pajama party.

Monday evening, as the party wound down, I found myself sitting alone with my biological mother as she packed. I had addressed her as "Aunt Lena" for years before learning her true identity. She owns the local psychiatric hospital and has become a management guru. We have little time together because our schedules often conflict.

"Ivan is the *second* person to declare that I must be Vladimir's daughter. His son was the first," I said, apropos of nothing.

My mother had been packing as we spoke and her hands froze in mid-air. A thought suddenly entered my mind. I tried to ignore it but couldn't. From the expression on her face, I *knew*.

"Vladimir *is* my father, isn't he?" I asked softly.

Though sensing this truth, I didn't want my mother to confirm it. My family relationships were complicated enough.

"I don't know," my mother said slowly, looking me directly in the eye and moving to sit beside me.

"My life was a mess when I lived in Europe. Both Peter and Vladimir were my lovers when you were conceived. Either could have been your father and I decided that Peter was the better choice. Vladimir is a good man—perhaps even a great man—but he had a family in Russia. I placed you with your aunt and uncle. You've had a loving adoptive family, and now love Peter and Vladimir too. Can you honestly say that I chose poorly for you?"

"No, you made a very good choice and have been a wonderful mother," I said, after only a momentary hesitation.

Then I remembered something.

"But you told me there had been a DNA test," I insisted.

"The DNA comparison was of mine and your's. Peter's DNA wasn't available. He had been long missing and the genetic material from his old personal objects wasn't suitable for testing. Biological evidence quickly corrupts in the warm, moist, English air.

"Peter's mother knew of my affair with him. It would never have occurred to one of her generation that I had another lover at the same time," my mother explained.

While we hugged, I couldn't help wondering if this knowledge would change my life.

www.ingramcontent.com/pod-product-compliance
Lightning Source LLC
Chambersburg PA
CBHW021945170626
46808CB00001B/27